CW00521400

ISEKAI MONSTER:

*Trying to be a Hero, When
Back Home You Were
Called a Monster*

By: Akos Esthoth

PROLOGUE

My name is Mikeal "Ash" Romanoff. In this world, I have a great destiny. That's right, "this" world. Ten years ago I was summoned to an alternative world as a "Hero". When I was summoned, there were already two other heroes here. An old guy who was the personal guard of the youngest royal child, a cute little princess and the other was the top general of the army, he was married to the king's younger sister, both of whom came from my world too. At first, I thought this would be a problem for my story; having other heroes already here, but both of them were nothing compared to me and my flames.

In books when people go to another world they're usually confused or scared, but not me, I was immediately looking forward to starting my protagonist lifestyle. This world gave me some cheat like magic that scoured the battlefield clean, leaving only ash. The war with the neighboring country I was summoned for ended quickly. However, before I could start my peacetime harem, demons attacked from the southern border. That war dragged on for years. Apparently, they were being led by a Demon Lord, typical. That Demon Lord ended up killing the hero General who I had heard was a big softy. It took some time, but I finished them easily; once they showed their face to me. The Demon Lord's ice magic was no match for my flames.

With the Demon Lord dead, the near-endless demon armies were forced to retreat. Having single-handedly saved this nation from back-to-back wars, they should have been bending over backward to reward me. That was just a few months ago, I no longer have the childish dream of a harem after years of war and countless women on the side. After over ten years here, that once little princess was looking ripe for a normal married life. So I thought maybe she could be my prize, heroes commonly marry royalty or nobles here, heck the first king and founder of this nation was apparently a "Hero." Yet, all anyone was talking about after the war was getting ready for the next hero summoning. Ten years went by so fast. I cannot even remember all the people I have killed in that time, only one other soldier had anywhere near my kill count, but they did not fight against the demons for some unknown reason.

That dunce of a king thinks some frontier land on the border is enough of a reward for summoning me and forcing me to fight in multiple wars. Even if it's prosperous land on the grain belt of the nation, ridiculous. The only other reward offered was my pick of any four castle maids to become my partners and aids in my territory. That bastard of a king was trying to get rid of me, sending me off to the boonies with only a few hotties. The old me might have jumped at that deal but I have fought for ten years for this kingdom and I want more than just wealth now. Also, not being offered the princess's hand just makes me all the madder. I am the protagonist of this story. I am supposed to get the princess and maybe even become king someday. If not for that old hero protecting the princess being called the Immortal I would have just stolen her. That kind of title might mean he is far older than he looks and I don't even know if my flames can kill him.

Luckily a bunch of nobles from the south also disagree with how the current king is running things, so I decided to help them out with a coup. Their personal forces are attacking and seizing key points around the capital and other areas. While I'm with the primary group of nobles directly attacking the throne room with the royal family and other heroes. They hired some assassins that will kill the king and the other royals in the castle before the coup even starts. Which should make everything go a lot smoother. My job is to suppress the new hero so we can blame him for the king's and queen's death to quell the populous. The new guy was only summoned a few weeks ago and while he is physically strong, he is weak compared to me. He doesn't even have any magic of his own, some people don't even think he's a "Hero." I mean he is strong, way stronger than a normal soldier or even me, but he has no magic, *yet*. For my part in all of this, I will get the first princess, become the new General Commander, and maybe even get the other princess too. After everything is over, I will seclude myself in my domain and the nobles will place some puppet such as the king's long-lost nephew on the throne. It is a brilliant plan if it works. If I play my cards right, I could end up king with a pair of princesses as my bride.

Unfortunately, even when everything is going according to plan, it can be frustrating. The day finally came for the coup and it all started without a hitch; Jin's plan went exactly as he said it would. However, the new "Hero" is a fucking worthless no talent; once the real fighting started, he froze up at the first sight of blood. The nobles said to be wary of him because he hadn't shown his unique magic yet, but a little bloodshed and he's trembling off to the side already. The knights on our side are negotiating with the minister and other high-ranking bureaucrats while he is just standing there mumbling to himself with this vacant look in his eyes. I thought he was better than this; when I saw him training, he looked very confident and sure of himself but now I know he was just putting up a front. Sure, it's only been a few weeks since he was summoned, but does he have to be such a fucking coward? His eyes are dashing around now, looking everywhere, frantically trying to find someone to save him and mumbling something incoherent under his breath. Suddenly his voice rises to an audible level.

"The princess escaped with the old Hero so even with the king and princes dead the kingdom will not collapse, now I just have to survive...... I guess that makes everyone in this room expendable." As he whispers that last part, his face and voice change completely. He no longer looks scared and fearful. No, now it is as if he lost all emotions and his voice almost becomes monotone. That eerily calm and emotionless voice silences the negotiating nobles. A few of them unconsciously reach for their weapons but don't draw them, seemingly out of fear as he continues.

"This narrative can work. All tragedies can be blamed on these fools and only successes will be attributed to me, the hero. Yes, that kind of story should work in any world, humans love a pleasant story." It takes me a moment to realize that it really is the timid hero who is still talking. The dissonance between his previous persona and now is too unsettling. This reminds me of horror movies from back home. That drastic change in tone of everything around you which tells the audience something terrible is about to happen. I can feel cold sweat running down my back. No, this is not a horror story, this is my story; I need to retake control of the situation, I am the hero here, I am the Red Knight, bringer of ash! His disturbingly calm voice breaks my concentration again.

"Hmm, how can I make this the most believable? Should I mutilate the corpses? Hey, minister of whatever. Of those who refuse to submit, would they mutilate your corpses before displaying them to the public?" That statement was too shocking, I could not even think of something to do before he started talking again. Everyone is too confused to make any kind of response until one of the old guys in the back answers.

"No, they would want the corpses in as pristine condition as possible. To better recognize them and show how merciful they were." That kind of thinking is so foreign to me I don't understand why that would matter. How would that show they are merciful?

"Oh, so that's how it works. It's good I asked, my narrative would have been to showcase their cruelty, but if that diverges too much from the expected reality then it won't be easily accepted." The tone of this conversation is completely at odds with its contents and the current situation, it's pissing me off and I'm not even sure why. Flames gather around me, it's my flame cloak, the searing temperature forces everyone away from me and even augments my physical abilities. This guy is getting out of hand, I need to put him in his place before this continues, I have to say something.

"That's enough out of you. Look around you. You have no allies and no escape option. Your only choices are to surrender peacefully or die." He slowly turns to face me. That look on his face is abnormally calm, and not the calm of someone who has everything under control. No, this is more like the calm of someone disinterested in what's going on around them, someone far above the situation like we are all just tiny ants to him. His attitude is rubbing me in all the wrong ways. My flames intensify, sending my allies scurrying to the other corners of the throne room. The floor melts beneath my feet, but his damn face is still a mask of calm and clear coolheadedness. It pisses me off to no end. He looks right at me with that face and says.

"You would normally be right, but that's assuming you and your lot are capable of subduing me. Though, I'll have to kill everyone here as my method of defeating you must be kept secret. With me as the only survivor, I open up a number of alternative paths, all of which still has me being the hero and you just a traitor to the crown." The way he says it even makes me believe he can do it for a moment. Only a moment. The other heroes couldn't do a thing against my flames. Even the Demon Lord of the Waning Crescent, who specialized in ice magic, couldn't stand against my fire.

The hardest part will be keeping his face recognizable, but we're going to kill him anyway so I will end him here and now. With a thought, I send a wave of fire to take out his legs to immobilize him and get rid of that smug look on his face. The flames crash against him and vanish as if hitting an invisible barrier; did his magic awaken or was he hiding it the whole time? The flames dispersed harmlessly. He is now wearing a cloak of shadows, much like my cloak of flames. I've never heard of a shadow or darkness element existing in this world's magic system. What is that? The only elements that could extinguish my flames are ice and water, and maybe a creative use of wind. I never got around to checking if conjured flames consume oxygen. A high-pitched shriek interrupts my thoughts. The high-priest who was hiding behind the hero is now trying to crawl further into the corner as he stutters out some words.

"D, D-D-DEMON!!!" The old man is frantically clawing at the walls as though he's trying to dig his way out of the room. His panic is rapidly spreading to the others.

"Don't bother. The room magically sealed itself the moment the king died. Only other royalty can deactivate the seal to enter or leave. That's why these guys have been so sure of themselves." Why does he know about the locking mechanism? He has only been here for a few weeks. I just learned that from the nobles to prepare for the coup. We were taking advantage of the fact that the hero would be sealed in here on the off chance his unique magic gave him the opportunity to flee. But why does someone just summoned to this world know the intricacies of royal magic? Another high-pitched scream interrupts my thoughts again. The old man who first shrieked has worn his fingers to bloody stumps as his frantic attempt to escape has sheared off his nails. Then I hear someone off to my side.

"It's the Demon Lord of the New Moon." This whisper is clearly heard coming from Joffrey, one of the nobles leading this coup. There is a sense of dread and hopelessness in his voice, as if he has already accepted death.

"When did you replace the summoned hero?" Joffrey pulls out his sword but is moving back, trying to put me in between himself and the new hero.

"An interesting misunderstanding has oc-

11

curred. Which confirms it was the right decision to hide my magic and that I can't leave any
witnesses." The hero is speaking with the same
unnerving calm despite the tension in the room
reaching greater heights. Even my hands are
beginning to tremble and he looks like he is about
to go to bed with not a care in the world.

"Well, time to get down to business." With
a wave of his hand, the shadows surrounding him
engulfs the people behind him and with a gasp,
they all collapse as if they were never alive to
begin with. Fear grips my heart for the first time
since coming to this world. Panicked, I turn my
flame cloak up to max power, disregarding the
safety of my collaborators. With another wave of
his hand, the shadows fly towards me. My flames
are extinguished instantly, one noble let out an
anguished gasp and everyone in the room but I and
the other hero fall to the ground. I can't properly process what is happening, is everyone dead
or asleep, is this really happening? Only Joffrey
showed any sign of pain. What is happening? Nobody looks like they died, they all look like they
just fainted, but I cannot help but think they are
already gone.

"Interesting, by enveloping yourself in
magic you managed to save your life. It would
be valuable to continue to experiment. However,
I apparently can't negate the heat from that pool

of lava you've created. So I'll end this now." The fool gave me the hint I needed. This brings me into a fighting state of mind, I channel my rage and indignation towards the ground. In less than a heartbeat, the pool of lava expands as a smile spreads across my face. This could work. I will cook him alive. As I contemplate how to handle all the dead nobles my mind blanks and I lose my breath. What was happening again? I can't remember what was going on just now or even who I am. What was I doing here, where is here? Then suddenly pain, unfathomable pain, it feels like my soul is being ripped from my body. Instinctually I try to scream but just a sigh escapes, and I fall to the ground.

The Fateful Encounter

The Twilight Kingdom, my home, is the most powerful nation in the world; our borders have not been rewritten in the last thousand years. That feat is made all the more relevant by the fact that we have been at almost constant war in those thousand years, fighting on one of three different sides of our territory east, west, or south. Until ten years ago we were in near-constant war with some small nation or another on our western side; the largest of which ended ten years ago when that nation dissolved and almost all of the land next to us is now considered a no-man's-land.

There are plenty of tiny villages to the west but no cities and no government binding them together anymore. I have heard that this has happened before about 600 years ago and they will probably form another nation, eventually. Likely a southern nation will interfere with them or some tiny village will grow into a veritable city and eventually a nation. However, we have never been the ones to start any of those wars and we would not even consider taking any of those vacated lands. No, our kingdom cannot bother putting too much thought and effort into our western side as we have been fighting against demons off and on along our eastern and southern border since our nation's founding.

I am the first princess of the Twilight Kingdom, Releina Maya Yuno la Twilight. This year during our sixth month I will turn 16 and today, the first day of the new year, I may be meeting my future husband. This meeting is rather late for a princess in our kingdom. Mother married father just before she turned thirteen. However, there are quite a few problems my father has had to deal with concerning my future. No, no, I will not be queen, I have two older brothers ahead of me in the line of succession, I also have a little sister. The problem for my late betrothal is two-fold; I defend the castle and cannot leave unless with my father. I am no mage, knight, or hero but I power all the magic circles that protect the castle, a hero once called me an infinite battery.

This was not always my job. My Mother, the Queen, protected the castle before but when my sister was born 8 years ago, she lost a lot of power and can no longer perform her duty. The king, my father, was going to call back some high mages back from the border with the demons to power the castle but the royal court mages in the castle determined that my power alone would be more than enough, much more actually. So I became a national treasure, in addition to a princess; incidentally, my younger sister is one as well and the two of us cannot leave the castle unless there are extenuating circumstances.

Normally I would have been married off to the hero that is summoned every ten years but the last hero summoned, the red knight, has a temper and is a bit unstable. Father doesn't even like having him live in the capital. He keeps trying to get him to move south by offering him the most valuable land in the kingdom to rule over and even his pick of the most talented maids in our service. Unfortunately, the red knight is not very intelligent and has some deeply concerning misconceptions of reality, but he is powerful so he has value.

The red knight has killed quite a few people for minor perceived slights against him, but father puts up with him because my uncle, the blue knight, died in the last war against the Demon Lord in the south. Uncle was such a kind man, I am told, after every battle he would cry with my aunt about having to take so many lives. He killed men in the war to the west ten years ago to protect her and the country, and it seemed even taking the lives of demons weighed heavily on him. Uncle was a "Hero" summoned 20 years ago, he married into our family soon after but it seems that he or auntie have some problems and could not have any children.

Many heroes marry royalty, however, because I am a national treasure the red knight cannot be trusted with me. So my father entrusted my future to his most trusted aid, our oldest hero. He was summoned 50 years ago, the white knight. He protects me and by virtue, the castle, as my personal knight. The white knight has the task of finding a proper husband for me, he is the one that set up my aunt and uncle so father trusts that he will find the most suitable partner for me. The two of them loved each other so much she passed not long after he did, offering herself to the next hero summoning.

For some reason, which I was never told, our oldest hero never married and seems to be dedicated to being a knight ever since he was sworn to my great grandfather when he was first summoned. I heard he had many friends in the knight corps and mage corps but they were only males so I don't think he has ever had any lover. His history was not that interesting, accomplishment wise, so I never bothered asking him or looking into it further than what he told me. He is always very professional with me; I think that is because he is wary of me like most people.

For the last few weeks I have been having dreams, even though I can never remember them completely, I am always happy when I wake up. They always begin with me being in a dark place then it is as if hundreds of lights get turned on far in the distance it almost looks like the night sky but I feel like they are eyes watching me, not stars. After I wake up Anna always says that I look happier than I have in years. Anna is my companion maid. She has been by my side since I was five. That vision is all I can remember from those dreams aside from the pleasant feeling. Now we come back to the meeting today, it has been ten years since the last hero was summoned which means it's time for a new hero to be summoned and this one just might be my destined one.

Now we come to what is currently happening. Around mid-day I head to the summoning room to prepare. My days are normally filled with studying and reading in the library. I would be training like everyone else if I was allowed to learn magic. Since I don't know summoning magic or any magic really I am simply the power source for the spell, or actually, my tutor said I was going to be the catalyst. Apparently, I am what is called a Furnace, it's hard to explain without an in-depth knowledge of magic so I don't really understand it myself. Magic has never been something I have been interested in since I was forbidden to practice magic not long after I was checked for my affinity. Essentially, I have so much mana I can't use normal magic; even the simplest of spells can go crazy if I try to use them. Once I tried a water spell with the help of one of the defensive circles after becoming the castle's defender, the spell flooded most of the castle city and damaged the circle.

The old man waiting for us in the summoning room is our royal court's only archmage. He is actually very excited about how different the summoning will be with my mana as the catalyst. As we reach the summoning room, the white knight opens the door for me and the old archmage is already waiting inside with an odd smile on his face. He is a rather old man, no longer the most powerful mage in the kingdom but still the most knowledgeable. He and the white knight have been friends for almost 50 years. Both of them were trained by my great grandfather 50 years ago when they were young, or so I am told. Almost all of my knowledge is second or third hand as I don't have full access to all the royal archives because my father is a worrywart.

"Ah princess we may begin whenever you are ready, the circle is finished I adjusted and widened it for you mana capacity. We may be able to summon from a world even farther away than normal, or perhaps even from the outside." The old mage laughs. He is one of the few people that can talk to me normally, even though he is just like everyone else. Distant and wary of me because of my personality and odd mana.

The old me would probably smile and respond with a comment following his flow to continue the conversation, but I stopped trying to hide who I am years ago. I am not quite sure what he means by that statement though. How many worlds are there? I don't remember any talk of that in any of my classes. It is hard to tell if he is going senile or actually has more knowledge that he has not told me yet. Father forbidding me from learning certain things is common so this could be part of that forbidden knowledge just like practical use of magic. The archmage Roland, this senile old man, is my tutor and he only teaches me general magic theory. Enough to use magic circles and power them for others to use or to activate automatically.

Father has decreed that teaching me anymore is far too dangerous, I always wonder if he thinks that way because of my mana or for other reasons, either way, I am forbidden from learning more, not that I cannot extrapolate far more than I am taught. That is why I tried using that circle once I was connected to it, however, it is obvious they were not lying; my mana is far beyond normal.

However, because I am not normal, some people look at me the same way they look at the red knight, even though I have never killed anyone. People give me looks that assume it is only a matter of time until I do. Never once have I had such a desire but just because I am different from normal people others are scared of me. The only people that dare to even touch my hand are Mother, Lilynette, my younger sister, and Anna, my companion maid who has been at my side since we were both children. The archmage Roland, white knight Suzuki, and my Father the king can talk to me somewhat normally but each of them are wary of me for different reasons. Also, I have never been close to my older brothers since they began military training while I was young and they have been stationed at various forts for the last eight years, they might not have even seen Lilynette now that I think of it. He looks like he is waiting for me to respond; I guess I should say something at least.

"Oh sir, you still have many secrets to teach me, don't you," I respond questioningly, yet knowing that he will probably never tell me everything I want to know. Such is the fate of royalty in the kingdom; we either fight at the front lines against the demons or work toward nurturing the next generation. All of us have much work to do on that front considering father lost almost all of his generation already. If I remember right, his only sibling still alive doesn't even live in the kingdom they ran off to the Republic of Kaar long before I was born; abandoning their right and duty to the throne.

"Yes, indeed princess, it will still take some time to teach you all that I know, hopefully, I live that long. Now we should begin soon if you please, the king is waiting for us." I want this over with as soon as possible as well. Just what kind of person will I summon? It is not impossible to get a woman, that has happened a few times in the past but it is rare.

After nodding to the old man, I move to the edge of the circle with the old mage and knight beside me. From this angle, I can see that even the walls have writing on them now, while only the circle in front of us is glowing the lines from it extend all around the room and even on to the ceiling. After I memorize the designs, I begin to pour mana into the circle. The circle begins to glow a dull green just like normal then the color changes like normal, the color that the circle changes to after green is what color the "Hero" is normally connected to and tends to become their knight title unless already in use. That color also hints at their unique magic, but not always. The circle changes to red and I become agitated. It's the same as the last hero, not good. Unexpectedly, the color changes again, this time to blue. The old man is rattled and raises his voice.

"This has never happened before!" The old mage cries. The color once again changes to yellow, purple, orange, and then back to green. This is getting interesting. I did not hold much hope for this hero, but this is not normal and I love it.

"This 'Hero' could be quite powerful and have many affinities." The white knight calmly says after the circle appears to stop changing color, but I can tell he is worried; his stance has changed into a defensive one.

The room starts to heat up and the color changes to white and gets brighter and brighter. It now hurts to look at the circle, I happily stare on not minding the pain. As it gets brighter, I feel my mana being drained from me at a rate unlike any-thing ever before; it is as if the circle is trying to devour me whole. In response to this, I unleash all the vast stores of mana deep inside me, like a dam bursting it rushes out of me. Roland once said that my mana alone was enough to kill a man if unleashed like this, I wonder if those two old men will die from me doing this? Hopefully, I will be able to call a hero that is perfect for me with this. The enormous ocean of mana that has filled me my entire life begins to drain. It is a euphoric feel-ing beyond anything I could have ever imagined; like a tremendous burden being lifted off me and something else flowing into me. The vast empti-ness that is engulfing me feels cool and familiar, a sweet embrace.

"Princess! Cover your eyes this could be dangerous, this heat is unnatural," The white knight yells and attempts to shield me, both him and the mage close their eyes and turn away from the glowing circle while trying to obstruct my view with their bodies. I can feel my eyes burning along with my heart. This is destiny, this "Hero" will be mine, I know it. Just as my vision begins to blur the circle becomes black, pitch black, and all the lights in the room are drawn into it, leaving us in complete darkness. Everything is dark then "he" is there; I cannot even see him at first, only feel his presence. Slowly the torch lights along the wall come back as if having their light returned to them, illuminating the room once more.

"It is over, the summoning is complete, what kind of hero did that ritual grant us?" The old mage begins to speak and opens his eyes. The white knight also looks on with wonder, then turns back to me and asks.

"Princess are you all right, quick Roland, heal her eyes quickly." The white knight yells at the old mage while I stare at "him" with blurry vision. As my vision slowly clears his form comes into focus as does my thoughts and my breath is stolen. In that instant, I see him and my blood runs cold, my face is flush, my spine tingles, I become light-headed, and yet I remain standing.

What is this feeling? Fear, love, hate, lust, anger, I have no idea. I have never felt like this, but I must regain control of myself. It has only been a few seconds but I need to start breathing again or I will collapse.

"Princess,"

"Princess, are you all right?" The two old men are trying to get my attention, but I cannot stop staring at that man. Yes, he is a man, not a boy or adolescent that are normally summoned. Neither is he an old man by any measure; he appears to have just entered manhood may be 20 at the oldest or he could be 16 and just matured faster than normal as I did.

This new hero is tall and handsome with some kind of formal wear on, it is as black as night just like his hair, giving his brown eyes an odd warmth to them. His clothes and hair are nice and orderly not hiding his face but his hair has a single short bang out-of-place making him look a little cute and not too stiff. The surrounding air is still. He has the look of someone who has seen war or has overcome many trials in their life. I can already feel a deep connection to 'him' as well as what is hiding deep inside him; an unknown strength, his mana, it has a frightening feel to it. Then he smiles at me, the first thing I think is that he is too perfect and after that so many other things begin to flow through my mind. I see so many possible futures for the two of us, too many. My thoughts and emotions overwhelm me. I forgot to breathe, didn't I? Unfortunately, this causes me to faint.

An Old Knight

White Knight of the Twilight Kingdom Suzuki Hanzou, I am the oldest serving hero in this kingdom. A former hero and king of this nation enlisted my service. He summoned me here 50 years ago when I was only 18. At the time there was only 1 other hero alive, Sir Siegfried, they summoned him over 50 years prior. This kingdom summons heroes every 10 years, but all the other heroes between my teacher and I had fallen to time or the most recent war with the Demon Lord to the east. His unique magic slowed the aging process to half, so he still did not look or act as old as he was.

That man died saving my life five years later, at the hands of the southern Demon Lord. I avenged him thanks to an opening that his death had created, but killing a Demon Lord is a hollow victory as they revive endlessly; though his death brought relative peace for 21 years. During that time I dedicated myself to protecting his family, the royal family for those 21 years. He was only the king for a brief time before giving his power to the previous queen and becoming a royal consort. She died several decades before him of old age.

At the time they summoned me, his grandson was already King. The grandson to that king rules the nation and I have the duty of protecting his oldest daughter and finding a man worthy of her and that can protect her; a herculean task. The perfect candidate would be a young hero, but the hero from 10 years ago is not worthy and there are none in the kingdom that can fill the task so I am laying a lot of hope on the 'Hero' we will summon this year. If he is not worthy, I will have to look outside the kingdom to find someone for the princess.

Most Heroes could easily fill the position, all the heroes summoned after I married into the royal family. The one called twenty years ago wed the current king's sister and led the nation's army as its general for years, but he fell recently against the revived southern Demon Lord just like my master. Our newest hero summoned ten years ago killed that Demon Lord so we should have peace for quite some time to come, but he is unstable. That man has no problem killing innocent people at the drop of a hat. We cannot trust that kind of loose cannon, I would have ended him years ago if we did not need his strength. Demon Lords can revive as early as 5 years after death; the last long peace from the demons was just luck. However, if the hero we summon today is strong, I can get rid of that foolish Red Knight Mikeal before he goes too far.

Today is the day; everything started off exactly as planned, I escorted the princess to the summoning room around noon. She is unusually happy today. She knows better than anyone that this hero could very well be her future husband. Seeing the normally reserved and proper princess like this is a sight for sore eyes. She has not acted like a normal girl since her older cousin left on a religious pilgrimage just after her younger sister was born. Even then she was lovingly looking forward to a new hero, I hope this one can live up to her expectations. We get to the room and I open the door. The archmage Roland has prepared a new summoning circle. He said earlier that he needed to adjust it for the princess's vast amount of mana. She is a very special existence that needs and deserves a hero to protect her as I will not be here forever.

Roland may be a doddering old man now, but he is a genius mage. Our master Sir Siegfried taught him many sciences from my old world. He may not be an excellent teacher, but he revolutionized our use of magic circles thirty years ago and has countless theories and formulas written in his office that I think even he has forgotten about. One of his favorite sayings to fresh recruits is, "I have forgotten more things than you will ever know."

Unfortunately, the summoning of the hero did not go as planned. From the moment the princess started, everything began down an odd path. The alterations that Roland did became apparent once she began pouring mana into the circle. He turned the entire room into a magic formula. I feared the summoning would fail, but after that blinding light, even though I could not see them yet, I could feel another hero. We summoned a youthful man no older than 25, if even that. He looks young and strong; he is wearing a black western style suit; it looks expensive. My world has likely changed a lot from when I was there, but only people of great standing or wealth wore these kinds of suits.

The first thing I notice after his attire is his mana. I feel mana from him, but it is condensed within him and not leaking out at all. How can he already have such control over his mana? Remembering that the princess was not shielding her eyes I immediately turned to check on her. She is shaking, her face is flushed and her eyes are red. She looks almost terrified, but also embarrassed? I have never seen her like this.

"Princess are you all right, quick Roland, heal her eyes quickly." The princess had stared directly at the circle while it was glowing with that bright light. I alert Roland of the princess's condition. We cannot have her fainting on us.

"Princess,"

"Princess, are you all right?" Both Roland and I try to get her to answer; but she is lost in his eyes? I have seen *this* look before; it is the same as the king's sister with the summoning 20 years ago. Well, that problem solved itself, but I would have never thought this princess would act so much like a normal girl. Then she collapses on the ground.

"Princess, Princess Releina please wake up," Roland calls to her and casts some restorative magic on her. After a moment she wakes up and I help her to her feet; all the while the summoned youth looks toward her with a concerning look but says nothing. Roland then turns his attention back to the youthful man.

"Hello, I am Roland the kingdom's High court mage. Hero, Welcome to the Twilight Kingdom." The youth looks calm; surprised but calm. That is expected all heroes are surprised when they are first summoned, a few even suffer fits of panic. He looks around as if trying to find his bearings, then turns to us and responds.

"It's a pleasure to be here. I am a bit dizzy so a place to rest would be nice, but let's take care of the formalities first. Who is in charge here?" He looks to the princess as he says this, it seems he said that out of concern for her since she did just faint.

"Of course, right this way, Hero." Roland led the way to the throne room. The way he is looking at the princess and that she is blushing so profusely, this looks perfect. It could not be going any better. Now he just has to be half as powerful as he looks and I can entrust her to him without regrets. We get to the throne room entrance; Roland speaks into the door and a moment later we hear the horn announcing the new 'Hero' to the kingdom and the door opens. It is during this time that I noticed how unflustered the hero has been. The princess's condition distracted me before, but now I realize it. He is far too calm, none of the heroes I have seen in all my time here have acted so reasonably; even I was in shock for days after getting here.

Before I can think of this more, the door fully opens and all of us enter the throne room. We need to let the king's court see the hero and send word to the church confirming the summoning. We proceed to the king's throne in the back of the throne room. The hero's posture has not wavered since we left the summoning room. He is not on guard but is definitely alert and is taking in all of his surroundings methodically. Like a trained soldier, what could his past have been? From his looks alone he is at most in his early 20s.

What could my old home be like now? Is he actually a trained soldier? Maybe he comes from an old noble or warrior family? Anything is possible. It has been fifty years, though, according to Mikeal, the world has been in relative peace since the cold war ended. Asking about home is a kind of taboo for heroes since we don't come from the same part of the world and the time difference. I only know what Mikeal offered in his introduction ceremony because he wanted to talk about his home a lot when he first came here. The king speaks.

"The summoning was an unprecedented success. I can feel an overwhelming power coming from you." The king can feel the same dense mana we all feel that seems trapped inside the hero. Wait, is it trapped in him? That could be bad. He might not have access to magic like this. That would be unprecedented, a 'Hero' without magic. That would be terrible.

However, all that mana I feel inside him. If it is truly trapped in him perhaps he could be strong and durable, like a permanent strengthening spell? I will have to test him once his training begins after he has acclimated to this world. That normally takes a month or two. The princess moves towards the king and takes her place beside him. I follow and notice the king glancing at her beat red face. He must wonder what is with his normally stoic daughter, but then his face changes as if he has realized everything and puts on a cheery grin and turns back to address the hero.

"Welcome hero, to my Twilight Kingdom. We have summoned you as part of our country's tradition of summoning heroes every ten years."

"Oh! Are you saying I wasn't summoned to fight a demon lord? Or a rampaging dragon? Or to end some war?" The hero looks shocked. His immediate response gives away that he had expected to have some grand quest given to him after getting here. He is a special summoning. Never has there been a hero called here knowing that they had a duty to fulfill. But he does not appear to be angry that there is no mission for him, just shocked. While they have never proven it, the church believes that every hero summoned either consciously or unconsciously agreed to the summoning, never has there been a hero that refuses his duty.

"Oh, well yes, the demons are a constant threat but we did not summon you to fix a specific crisis. A hero long ago set up the system to periodically summon heroes so they are ready when a disaster strikes. However, our nation is not in the middle of a crisis. It is a very rare occasion in our history, but we are at peace."

The king responded a little hesitantly, trying to reassure the hero he has a mission waiting for him. The young hero looks puzzled. Did he accept the summon because he knows of a pending crisis? What if this unique hero was summoned to deal with an equally unique problem? Dammit, if he has come because we are heading to dismal times I cannot look forward to a peaceful retirement. Dammit, I cannot get rid of that accursed Red Knight now either. If we are heading for troubled times, we will need all the power we can get. Ah, some time has passed while the young hero is thinking and the king looks concerned.

"If you are worried about how you will be cared for, worry not. You will live in the castle and be instructed in magic and martial arts before being given a noble rank and land to manage if you so desire. You will be expected to fight for the nation and its people against demons or foreign invasions. Oh, we seemed to have skipped the order of some things but could we have your name Hero." The young hero looks directly at the king and proudly says.

"I am Seigi", I flinch, this cannot be a coincidence. That name is in my native language, I did not even realize until now because of what happened to the princess. This man, no Seigi, is Japanese. Just like me. How could I have not noticed that before? I know none of the other heroes in this kingdom are from Japan and none of the ones I know of outside our nation are. However, considering this man and that name, tragedy lies ahead of us. I must protect the princess at all costs.

"Seigi. All right, please show Seigi to his room; he'll begin lessons tomorrow if he is up for it. Mia, you will look after Sir Seigi and see to his every need." Roland and Mia take the hero away, while I head to escort the blushing princess back to her room to rest. It is not late, but today has exhausted her. After bowing to a smiling King and Queen, I follow her with the future weighing heavily on my mind.

Once he is up for it, I will have to push Seigi to see just how strong he is and if he can use any kind of magic. Normally I would not even think of starting training that intense, so early, but I have a feeling that he will be up to the challenge. Judging by his gait he has had some kind of formal training, likely some form of martial arts. Oh, I wonder if he knows how to use a Katana? That might be bad; they don't have swords that good here. Perhaps another country does, I will have to ask Roland to look into that for the future. Unfortunately, I only see black clouds ahead of us.

Our Hero

Life is hard. I don't mean to say I am suffering undue or excessive hardships. Simply that living a normal life is filled with difficulties. Take today, for example. I was placed in charge of a new division this morning. That sounds like a splendid thing and I am expected to be happy about it, but it's filled with more problems than benefits. I'm in charge of more people than before, and a lot of valuable equipment. Unfortunately, most of them are incompetent because the competent ones keep getting promoted. I have one week to rid myself of dead weight and shift their duties to the remaining few. Then I have to look for people to replace those that I let go, all while keeping up with my father-in-law's expectations.

But, I hear you say, a promotion may mean more work but it also means more pay and more pay is always better. That is not true. My account is already steadily filling with extra cash that I could enjoy spending, but with working well over sixty-hour weeks their best use is to sit in an account until I need it. So no amount of pay can compensate for more work because while time is money, money isn't time. Not that I would spend it, anyway; I am not one to spend money on entertainment.

No, I would likely use it on Haruno or invest it for our future, although, I think she is already doing that. I am glad that she has a clear vision for our future, one less thing I have to focus on. Finding her was a stroke of luck for me, she removed many variables from my future many years before I even had to worry about them. Ever since I met her, life has been far easier than before. Making her happy is far better than dealing with uncertainty. I will always be grateful to her for that.

That is the biggest problem today. However, another one I've pushed back repeatedly has been forced onto today as well. I can no longer ignore this social engagement so the last vestiges of my time are eaten up yet again. Yet it still gets worse. Despite having scheduled this dinner for other reasons, because of my promotion it will now become all about me and I will be forced to reschedule a new dinner to replace this one. I could hide my promotion, but that is asking for more problems by keeping secrets. The kind of problems I don't need. That is not the person I am, I already know all of those possible outcomes so I just have to follow the most logical path like always.

Yet, this is the life I have chosen. I regret nothing. This is just what it means to be part of modern human society. Ever since that incident

10 years ago I have been working toward this, a normal life, no one will call me that again. Still, I wonder if everyone works this hard to be normal, to be happy? No, I know that most do not, I would never have been labeled as such if that were true. I must be vigilant, the only way to be happy is to be accepted, being unique is accepted but only to a degree so I must soldier on this path. All the expectations people have for me that are within reason I will meet and even exceed some of them; within the margin of error, of course. I will not let Haruno cry like that one did; our future is set, even this latest promotion was within expectations. So I will continue down the path I have forged for myself, ready for anything that could logically happen.

Huh.... I'm disorientated. I'm down on a knee and the world is spinning despite the uniformity of the darkness surrounding me. Calm down, panic is the enemy. What is my current condition? My hand opens and closes as I quickly assess my situation. I have all of my fingers and don't register any pain, but I feel warmer? It is odd, but it feels almost like when you're in a hot spring, soothing heat, but it's coming from inside me, not enveloping me like a hot spring. I'm kneeling in darkness and don't remember at least the last few minutes.

Okay, then let's construct those missing

memories, what is my last memory? I was walking down a semi-busy street in Tokyo at night. When there was a sudden flash, almost like lightning. Was there a sound? I don't remember a loud noise. The most likely scenario is the flash was an explosion from a terrorist attack. The flash has either permanently or temporarily blinded me. Wait, I don't hear any panic. So I've gone deaf as well. That is disappointing. Fortunately, the medical technology father-in-law's company is working on should be able to eventually fix any damage I might have taken from a bomb. The fact that I don't feel any pain is concerning; this might be something else entirely.

If this is my condition, my first step should be checking on my companion who was on my right. I grope around in the dark and notice the texture of the floor is wrong. The concrete sidewalks are very familiar and this is nothing like them. I need to reevaluate. The ground feels like polished stone. The air smells stagnant, like a room that's been locked for months or years. I hear a gasp and air moving. I haven't lost my hearing. I probably haven't lost my sight either. The room is just dark, but let's not jump to conclusions.

After a bright light, I was transported, unharmed, to an unfamiliar location. Corporate spies could have kidnapped me. While possible, the fact that I am unbound and uninjured makes this impossible. There is no other reasonable explanation for this event, yet here I am. Let us check the unreasonable to be ready for anything. First unreasonable option, I somehow got blackout drunk at dinner and have just now awoken. Second, a secret government research facility that has been experimenting with teleportation had a mix-up in the coordinates that somehow resulted in moving me to the intended location.

Neither makes the least bit of sense. While I don't hold my alcohol well, I am quite aware of this, meaning I would have been tricked or forced to drink to excess. No one around would have done such a thing and even allowing that unlikely event; waking with no injury and all of my clothes is pushing the unbelievable too far.

As for a teleportation accident. I know many companies are working on that technology, but none I know of are anywhere close to practical testing. It's possible mine is the first accident, so no one has heard of them. It would also explain my dizziness and otherwise pristine condition. However, why am I in a pitch-black room? A target room would be well lit and well monitored. It's possible to go further down an unlikely path and say I was unintentionally grabbed and then flung somewhere unintentional. However, that begs the question of the likelihood of landing in a perfectly dark empty room and not in a wall or in space.

Logic doesn't support my current reality. So I guess I roll with the situation as it unravels. As I am thinking I notice the presence of 3 people in this room, maybe this is a target room or holding facility, researchers then or kidnappers? Lights seem to turn on along the wall. What? Torches? And they turned on automatically? No, those are not flames emitting light, maybe just custom LEDs, I would have to get a closer look to be sure. What are my options, escape, or cooperation? Is there any middle ground? I could reasonably take down two people but if they are trained guards I might struggle against two of them.

Resisting is a last resort at the moment. Having decided on my course of action, I stand up and make myself presentable. As I raise my body, it feels lighter almost nonexistent. Is gravity weaker, are we in space, am I just light-headed, what does this mean? The ground feels odd too; its texture was that of stone but the resistance I feel is almost like foam. If I tried I could push my foot into it easily, very odd.

The three individuals in here with me are in odd postures as well, all of my ideas are looking less and less likely. An old man in a worn-out robe is hiding his face and turned away as if hiding from a bright light. Did they see the light too? There is another old man in armor, a knight? He is in a similar posture, looking away from me. Are they cosplaying? The one in armor looks Japanese. They are both flanking a young European looking girl with blond hair in a plain white dress and shining silver eyes.

Oh no, she is staring right at me, her eyes are reddened. Was she looking at the light? She looks scared; she is trembling and her face is blushing too. Oh no. I dropped it, damn; I dropped the mask that I have had for five years because of the disorientation and shock. I dropped it, this is why I don't drink, she is terrified of me now just like those others ten years ago.

"It…. is….. over,……. the…. summoning…….. is…. complete,……. what….. kind….. of…... hero…... did….. that….. ritual……. grant…... us?????" The old man in robes starts talking but why is he talking so slow and their movements; it is all in slow motion.

I can understand them, but what I hear doesn't match what it looks like they are saying. Did he say 'Hero?' Oh no, like those stories. I never thought of that, cosplayers are looking increasingly less likely. Do I roll with this as well? Could they be a cult? If so, how dangerous would it be to resist their narrative? At the very least I need to see a method of escape before I become hostile or uncooperative. Ok, cooperation, what will work best here. Arrogance? Submission? They called me a hero so I don't want to be too meek. And heroes shouldn't be rude either. Let's go with confident, polite neutrality.

"Princess, are you all right, quick Roland, heal her eyes quickly." The knight turned to the girl and began yelling. I guess she is a princess and that old mage looking guy must be Roland.

"Princess,"

"Princess, are you all right?" They are both yelling now. They said heal her, I bet they mean to use magic. If it is like those stories what should happen now? Maybe I should have read some of those stories, nothing to do about that now.

To think of something, this out of the ordinary would happen to me. Now they seem to be speeding up, or am I the one slowing down. Either way, this is better. Now the girl, what to do about her? She still looks scared of me. If she has not seen my face before I could have used one of my normal faces but I guess I have to go with number 5. Yeah, it is all I can do, the worst case is that it ends the same as last time but she won't be scared anymore and that is more important. So I show her my smile and then she faints. Of course, it is the worst case, but that problem can be pushed off until later.

"Princess, Princess Releina please wake up," The old man, Roland, calls to her and his hand lights up, that must be magic. After a moment she wakes up and the knight helps her to her feet. After confirming that she is fine, Roland then turns his attention back to me,

"Hello, I am Roland, the kingdom's high court mage. Hero, Welcome to the Twilight Kingdom." Yeah, I figured this is one of those stories, this is just perfect. Right when I had my life already set. I kind of wish I read some of them. All the knowledge I have is second hand, so then I have to treat this just like ten years ago. Stay calm, gather what this culture's social cues are and fit in, so let's begin.

"It's a pleasure to be here. I am a bit dizzy so a place to rest would be nice, but let's take care of the formalities first. Who is in charge here?" With that, I can show concern for the princess and let them know that I am a kind-hearted, caring hero, although she will not like that. Considering how she is blushing, she knows why I said that. Well then, I cannot let my mask drop again. It could have ruined everything I have done up till now. Although all that work seems to have been for nothing. If this really is another world, everything before now was for naught.

"Of course, right this way Hero," The old man leads the way. The girl is trembling, she doesn't seem to be taking this well, she must be really embarrassed. I'm led out of the room and through a number of hallways. Everything is stone, which gives it a medieval vibe but the torches along the walls look like they have LEDs on the top, and the floor feels soft like memory foam, I wonder if I push on it would it return to its normal shape. I haven't passed a single window. How do they keep this ventilated? I can feel a breeze, but it's coming from the walls. They have integrated air conditioning? Nothing is making sense. The more and more unlikely is becoming reasonable. We stop at a large ornate door and Roland moves next to it and whispers.

"The summoning was a monumental success. The new hero is impeccable and powerful. Let the kingdom know and I will give the king a full report after the introduction, the ritual exhausted the princess, we need to finish fast."

Roland seems to have been whispering, but I heard everything loud and clear. I could never hear whispers that clearly before. This, that constant warmth, and the weakened gravity. I must have changed when coming here. I have to be careful about this, it could not be normal, I will need to see how everyone acts here before I make some enormous mistake again.

A blaring horn breaks the silence. The door opens not to another hallway but a massive room. This is definitely a throne room, there is no other name for a room that draws all attention to an overly ornate chair. A man probably in his late fifties sits on the throne with a look of anticipation. On a smaller throne right next to his is a woman who looks to be in her mid-twenties. She's barely older than the girl next to me. Could she be the queen? If she was his daughter she would sit on a lower stair, right? Not next to him. Is this normal?

Should I comment or ignore this? This is a king. Should I kneel or bow? I think I missed my chance for either. There are about ten other people in the room as well; all standing along the walls. Some women in maid attire and a few men and women in Victorian era looking outfits. Likely the king's court; high-ranking nobles or family members, everyone seems to have been waiting for me. This is a major event; I have to be wary.

We all stop right in front of the king. This would be the time to bow or kneel, right? However, I am supposed to be a hero. Also, they might not have that sort of custom here. Since I don't have some frame of reference, I will do neither. The others don't make any kind of show of respect, perhaps this kingdom doesn't show respect that way. This is another world and all cultures even back home have different standards. I have to observe everyone so I can match them just like always and then take into consideration what being a hero means.

In the stories I have read one does not become a hero until they have saved a princess, killed some monster, or ended some kind of conflict, however, here I am already a hero to them. Yes, those sent to another world stories work differently, you call a hero to complete one of those tasks. Meaning I am going to have some kind of job given to me. That will not be so bad, choosing your own path can lead to unforeseen problems; having one set out for you could be a tremendous boon. Even back home my path was set once I met Haruno. I did not have to choose randomly, I just ended up working for her father.

"The summoning was an unprecedented success. I can feel an overwhelming power coming from you." The king is practically jumping for joy as he looks at me. Am I radiating an observable aura? Do people here have some sixth sense, is it the warmth within me?

That is the only thing different about me

that others would be able to notice. There is no way other people could tell if my body feels different from before, they would have no reference, so that must be it; people here can sense this warmth in others. Though I cannot feel anything from these people that resembles that warmth, is it a hero only thing? No, most likely I just don't have that ability, which means I am going to be at a disadvantage from the start. Looks like I might have to guess that stuff based on other people's reactions.

No one here is hiding their emotions but they could be faking it like me, the old Japanese knight is the only one here even suppressing them at all. Everyone in this room is noticeably happy; this society just seems more open about those things than back home. Reading people here looks like it is going to be easy, life here might be easier than back home. The princess shuffles her way up to the throne with the knight close behind her. After the princess gets in her position, the king gives the knight a knowing, and smiles, then he continues.

"Welcome hero, to my Twilight Kingdom. We have summoned you as part of our kingdom's tradition of summoning heroes every ten years." What? A tradition? Meaning there are other heroes? Potentially a lot more.

"Oh! Are you saying I wasn't summoned to fight a demon lord? Or a rampaging dragon? Or to end some war?" I leaped before I looked. That answer surprised me a bit. This is not how I remember those stories go. Normally there is only one hero summoned from what I remember. Not good, how can I spin this. How was that perceived? Was I overbearing?

"Oh, well, the demons are a constant threat but we didn't summon you to fix a specific crisis. A hero long ago set up the system to periodically summon heroes so they are ready when a disaster strikes. Our nation is not currently in the middle of a crisis. It is a very rare occasion in our history, but we are at peace." The king seems a little shaken to have been interrupted, but he's taken it as a reasonable response. I haven't blown it yet. Let's look at my situation then. If they make a habit of summoning heroes and have them live here, then they probably don't have a method of sending them back.

I guess all that work before was for naught. No, not completely. It proved that I can live a normal life, I will just have to start from scratch. This world is unfamiliar but they appear human and act similarly; all I can do is live my life. As for a future crisis; it seems that in this world it's more a matter of when not if like home. That could be dangerous and since I am a hero now, I will have to deal with whatever problem comes up. I am going to need to learn about this world fast. The king begins again, interrupting my thoughts.

"If you are worried about how you will be cared for, worry not. You will live in the castle and be instructed in magic and martial arts before being given a noble rank and land to manage if you so desire. You will be expected to fight for the nation and its people against demons or foreign invasions. Oh, we seemed to have skipped the order of some things but could we have your name Hero."

So they have a plan all ready for me and as I thought something will happen. I am going to be trained in magic and martial arts that most likely means the sword. Magic, that could be interesting; learning new things always came naturally to me, one of the few things I enjoyed. Now about a name; I can just make one up. He is asking for my name but never mentioned his, no one here has said their name either, normally one introduces themselves first. As king maybe he does not have a name anymore or just none of us can use it? I hate not knowing the proper etiquette, better off not bothering asking his name, it might be rude. Now, I never liked my old one, not since that incident. 'Yuusha' seems like I am pushing it, then there is just one choice.

"I am Seigi." The old guy with the princess twitches at my name. Yes, he is definitely Japanese and knows what that means.

"Seigi." The king says the name I gave as though tasting its flavor.

"All right, please show Seigi to his room; he'll begin lessons tomorrow if he is up for it. Mia, you will look after Sir Seigi and see to his every need." Training should be a perfect method to figure out how people interact here. I was department head for 9 hours, now I'm in an alternative world dealing with an unfamiliar culture as a hero. Life is hard.

What Happened Afterward

"Everyone has left the room, your Majesty," A guard informs the king.

"My queen, what do you think?" The king asks with worry in his voice.

"That was different. He seemed to have a purpose to all his actions and did not ask many questions, almost like he was expecting this. From what I remember of the records, no hero has acted like that before. Almost universally Heroes show some confusion, doubt, or even denial of what has just happened to them. His name was the only information about himself he gave willingly, perhaps because that was all you asked of him?" That was how the Queen responded, then the king interrupts.

"Yes, sir Suzuki noticed it too. That young man, Seigi, has a purpose. It may not be some kind of mission that needs to be done, but he is driven. If we had asked him more about himself, he most likely would have answered, but I think we can leave that to Releina. This may mean we are in for disastrous times, but Releina seems instantly taken with him. I cannot recall a time I have seen her so flustered, it reminds me of how young she still is. Yes, since Venus left, I have not seen her show anything other than disdain for others."

"Your Majesty if I may." The old mage Roland speaks up.

"The summoning was quite different this time as well. The circle shifted color many times; to all the known colors and ended with a bright and hot light. It was completely unprecedented, the amount of mana the princess used was almost equal to what the summoning crystal provided. Truly this was a miracle similar to the first's summoning."

"Then I have decided, send word to border forts, we have summoned a new hero and we are to heighten alert levels. Have them all double scouting missions for the foreseeable future. Roland, I charge you and Suzuki with Seigi's training. He will take lessons with Releina starting tomorrow; I am sure he will be willing. Mia will give daily reports on his mental health. I will retire to my room for the rest of the day; I need to think of the future, my queen will you accompany me?" A nod from the queen and then the two of them leave together arm in arm. The last word before everyone else left the room where Roland's.

"I guess things will get very busy from now on, I hope these old bones hold out."

Princess Releina's Room

I am Anna, the first princess's handmaid, she and I have been together since we were 5. The princess has two other maids but those positions change every few years. I am the only one who has been with her since she left the nursery. We have known each other before that, but I was not a maid then and we would rarely talk or play together before that. Since we left the nursery we have been through all kinds of hardship and illness. There is no one I am closer to than her. Though we are not friends, she is the first princess; I have been the only one she can talk to about her problems. Even if we are the same age, I feel like a big sister to her and want to help her, but I have never seen her like this.

Princess Releina was so happy today, that itself was unusual, but everyone knew why. Today was the summoning of the new hero and she would most likely marry that hero. So you can understand that none of us can understand why she is in her bed crying her eyes out, she won't say anything, she is just crying. The other maids pushed me in here to find out why. I want to comfort her, but I have never seen her like this. It is odd seeing her act so much like a normal girl.

If she was just upset I could deal with it like I normally do by comforting her, but I don't think that will work this time. I slowly make my way to her bed. While she has never once been violent, Roland was firm in his warning that if her mana goes out of control, it could kill us even if we guard with our own mana at full power. That is just how much mana she has, no one person is a match for her.

"Princess Releina, please stop crying, if there is anything I can do please let me know. If you would like me to comfort you I am here for you any time." I plead with her, trying to get some kind of response, but all I hear is her sobbing. Now that I am closer to her I can tell her mana is under control. It is shocking I couldn't feel it until now. Normally you can feel her mana anywhere in the castle. The summoning must have taken a lot out of her. Could that be why she is like this? I move closer now that I am sure it is safe.

"Were there some problems with the new hero? We all heard the horn announcing the successful summoning." With that, she stops crying and lifts her head out of her pillow, then looks at me with a terrible face and cries.

"The hero thinks I am a child." She then

grabs onto me and continues to cry while telling me what happened.

"I fainted, I fainted! He smiled at me and I just collapsed. When I first saw his face I thought my heart would stop, I stopped breathing. The very definition of masculinity, handsome face but clean-shaven, well-toned and muscular body and the air of battle around him; but his smile was so kind and soft. He was so regal, a true hero, much stronger than the red knight, more caring than my uncle, and he even had a kingly aura rivaling if not exceeding my father; the perfect hero.

And I fainted at his smile, then out of concern for me, he did not even ask many questions of my father regarding the summoning just to let me rest. He must think I am nothing more than a child that needs to be protected! That is the problem!" She screamed that last part. Oh my, this is a problem. One that I never thought I would have to deal with either, but I guess she is more normal than I thought.

"Princess, if he is truly as you say then it is only natural for you to faint, could you have ever thought of meeting such a man before seeing him? Honestly, I cannot wait to see him, hopefully, after hearing about him from you I might be able to hold myself together." A little perspective should get her to realize the situation is not as bad as she thinks. At least not yet, if she continues to act like a child she really will only be seen as one.

"That makes sense," Releina lifts her head, still sobbing slightly.

"But not if he shows you that same smile. Just thinking about it now, ah." The oddest smile appears on her face as she remembers. She gets lost in her thoughts like this constantly; ignoring the rest of reality while she explores possible futures in her mind. Once I had her explain what she is doing while she is lost, apparently she is running simulations. It is something she does unintentionally once she has an interesting thought in her head she runs with it.

"Princess you need not worry. Steel yourself for the future; I am sure he will have to train and learn magic, as all the heroes do. Perhaps he will have lessons with you." The princess turns back to me with a stern face and replies,

"It would not surprise me in the least if he needs no training and even knows magic already. However, no matter how perfect he is, he will have to learn our history and common knowledge. I must be the one to teach him, I am sure father will allow it, and that old mage knows nothing besides magic." Releina jumps out of bed and goes to her bookshelf and pulls one of them out.

"This will be perfect, 'The founding of the Twilight Kingdom' a basic outline of our history starting with the first hero, no, I am sure this book will be in his room. He will most likely try reading everything he can once he gets there, and the translation skill heroes have should allow him too. No, no, I will have to do a report of our most current information so he can have a good grasp of our situation.

Anna, you and the other maids go to all the ministers and ask for written summaries of their most recent works. I want to know everything that is going on in the capital tonight and the rest of the kingdom by next week at the latest. This will show I am not some wallflower nor a child, I am the first princess. I need to calm down and get to work, what are you waiting for Anna, go tell the others there will be no sleeping tonight we have to help prepare for the future." Now, this is the princess I know, mature beyond her years, I must help her anyway I can.

"Yes princess, I am off." I head out to complete my mission; it will be an arduous night. The King limits what we teach Releina. However, I think I can get past the normal restrictions. If I ask Shanna, my older sister, she can get me some classified information. Even just a little more information and Releina will extrapolate what is missing. She is far more intelligent than her parents give her credit for.

Releina could always tell when the red knight was acting odd and would likely blow his top. She told her father that he would kill someone close to him and to not give him a personal maid. When Lilynette's power awakened, confirming her as a saint, she also warned that the red knight was a dangerous existence and they need to be wary of him. I wonder if Lilynette also gave her parents an oracle about Releina's future?

Seigi

I woke up the next day to an unfamiliar ceiling.

"I guess it wasn't a dream." Not that I thought it was, I have never had any dreams that I can remember.

Last night I figured out a few other things about this nation and this unknown world I am stuck in. After looking through all the books in my room I noticed something, while they were not in Japanese I could read all of them easily. Everything, whether it is what people are saying or what I am trying to read, is being translated for me but not into a language I know. It is not translated into a language I know; somehow I just know what someone says or writes. The book I ended up reading all of was a children's storybook about the founding of the kingdom.

It read similar to how I assume those other kinds of hero stories go. Someone transported to an alternative world and they use their special magic and knowledge of their world to bring peace and prosperity to the land. Because of this, they summon heroes every ten years; they bring some new knowledge, but they do it mostly for the heroes to be warriors. Also, more than half of them marry into the royal family so my problem with the princess might not be one.

The demons that they fight against are seen as a natural disaster; at least from the perspective of this children's book. They attack every decade or so; from either the south or east and on the rarest of occasions both. The book did not have many details about them, but that might also be because they know little about them. One of the oddest things that the book noted was that the demons don't really try to take territory and they attack in almost preset numbers of a couple thousand at a time and within only certain hours of the day.

Never once have they attacked at night and even when they overrun an outpost or fort they leave it come nightfall. This nation's militaristic nature also seems to be a major factor, every citizen has mandatory military training and unless given a pass by royal decree, serve ten years in the army.

Even royalty and nobles fight on the front lines regardless of wealth or gender. They even appear to be some of the most powerful soldiers, not counting the summoned heroes. From what the book said, the only people that tend not to fight on the front are some princesses as they marry young and raise many children. It also seems that having a king rule the nation is a rarity as they tend to die in battle; only ones that live to an old age rule for lengthy periods of time. For most of this kingdom's history, queens have ruled over it until their children come of age. At which point they transfer power over to the next generation.

The current king looked kind of old; at least compared to the other people I have seen, but I would not place him over sixty years old. So he retired from the battlefield and got himself a young queen? However, his queen looked too much like the princess to not be related. She could be her mother and just ages more gracefully than that old man. Although the queen and princess don't look like they have trained a day in their lives. They must do some other job which would exempt them from military service.

As for why this kingdom is still in a pre-industrial era, even with advanced knowledge and magic. The first reason is that magic isn't some kind of fix-all, do anything you want power. According to this book, it has some very real limitations and can vary wildly even between people of the same family. Second, the demons are a constant and never-ending threat to humanity; even the weakest demons are immortal. Taking anywhere from less than a year to a decade to revive. Demon Lords are as strong or stronger than most

AKOS ESTHOTH

heroes and that power changes their respawn rate by a factor of ten, but their individual power changes that rate even further.

The Demon Lord of the Waning Crescent, the one that is constantly attacking this country from the south, has a revival rate of ten to thirty years, seemingly dependent on how she died. One instance has her head being cut off, and she revived in ten years. Another has her being completely annihilated and not returning for almost fifty years. All the demon lord's names are from the moon phases, but this book doesn't have much detail about the rest of them since it is for children.

This nation is located in the northern center of the continent, the whole landmass is shaped like a diamond, but it says here that the maps are not accurate. The near isolationist policies that govern this kingdom means they know little about the southern human nations. Aside from the fact that the largest nation in the south, Sow, hates them and warred with them almost constantly over six hundred years ago until some large-scale disaster happened.

Considering it is demon territory to the south. I can guess the disaster involved them. To the north is the endless sea, to the south and east is demon territory, and even though they don't fully

64

trust their maps it looks like this diamond-shaped continent is like two puzzle pieces. With the protruding area being controlled by the demons; aside from that, it looks like the whole continent is half controlled by demons and half by humans.

Though the east has only invaded every fifty years those wars last for quite a while only ending with the Demon Lord of the Waxing Crescent dying along with several heroes. It is very possible he has not revived, and that is why the east has not moved in so long. Records show that there have been a few times he has taken almost a century to revive.

Finally, the west is human territory; many smaller nations that rely on us for protection from the demons are among them. Some kingdoms almost as big as us are farther to the west some of those even have their own heroes. Far south-west is a large mountain range, a small dwarven nation controls the most northern mountains. Though small in population they control an extensive area of land according to this map.

This book has little information on them, I hope that is not the same for the state. The nations farthest from us; beyond the dwarves' mountains are unknown. The map shows that the mountain range branches off to the west and south, isolating the lands beyond it. Likely only the nations right next to those mountains have any knowledge of what is in the valley beyond those mountains. There is also a note here that the demons attack every other coastal nation we know of, but not once in the last eight hundred years have they been attacked from the sea to the north.

There is no knowledge of island nations and ships from every nation cannot venture too far from land, but not because of the demons, there are gigantic sea monsters that even the demons fear out beyond what is logically a steep continental shelf. Things like monstrous leviathans, terrifying kraken, and island turtles could run rampant in the endless sea.

All human nations belong to a group similar to the United Nations; this group handles problems through negotiation with little to no fighting. It was created six hundred years ago but doesn't have much genuine power since wars break out all the time still. The major function they perform is organizing the smaller nations so they can summon heroes to defend their borders. All the larger nations help at their leisure, which seems to be the primary reason it lacks proper authority to do anything about infighting between the largest nations. So much like the UN back home, though it has existed for so long it has to be doing something right.

It also seems the church aids them with the most severe emergencies. During those times when a nation is on the brink, if the church sees fit they will send their own heroes to give aid. That sounds odd, the church is not a nation, but it has its own heroes? It also seems that they collect saints from every nation to do the work of the seven, around all of human territory. There is no other information on the Church of the Seven in this book aside from the fact that it was established twenty thousand years ago by the eternal king of the night.

After finishing that book it seemed to only be around midnight and I did not feel tired at all but figured I should rest for tomorrow's training. I woke up just as the sun was coming up feeling refreshed. The maid, Mia, they assigned to me doesn't appear to have slept at all and is waiting for me in the room's corner. She appears to be 20ish, long black hair, above average chest, the kind that would have made her very popular back home and what I assume to be an attractive face based on reasonable aesthetic appreciation. I don't think she is supposed to watch me like this though.

At first, I showed her my number 2 face yesterday when she was introducing herself to me and she almost fainted. Women here seem to have no resistance at all, or is being a hero adding some kind of strengthening? Number 2 never got that kind of reaction back home. It was my default for introductions. A warm, welcoming smile. This could very well become an enormous problem for me, but I already know how to fix it. The plan is the same as back in my world, unless social norms are different here. Damn, I will have to find out about that before dealing with this. Creating a harem is not something I plan on doing unless I am forced to, that is just too many variables to deal with.

"Mia would breakfast now be too early or do you think I should wait," I asked while using face number 7, she jumped at my question. I wonder if she was sleeping with her eyes open?

"I will see Seigi-sama," With that, she leaves the room with a bow. I head to the counter where a water basin is, to give myself a rubdown to start my day.

The door opens, I hear a gasp, a squeak, and a thud. Knocking is not the norm here, it seems. Mia has returned with the princess and who I assume is her maid based on her attire being the same as Mia's. They must have run into each other in the hallway. The princess is on the floor. She fainted again and her maid is beet red but attempting to rouse her with what must be magic

again. Not letting her rest and waking her immediately seems odd. Wouldn't it be best to take her
back to her room?

I wonder if she has some condition or just
cannot be left unconscious? The princess's maid
resembles her in a way that makes me think she is
her body double; their figures are evenly propor-
tioned, hair color and even their faces are similar.
Everything the same or similar aside from their
eyes. The princess has unnatural silver eyes that
shine in the right light and the maid has dull gold
eyes or amber. In any case, I put my shirt back on
and by then they had revived the princess

"Seigi-sama breakfast has been prepared
and once we are finished you will have magic lessons with me and sensei if you are up to it. I also
have reports on the most current situation of the
kingdom and the surrounding nations to go over
with you after that. Then, spirit willing, Sir Suzuki," the princess gestures behind her, the old
knight from before is in the hallway, "will begin
sword training if needed."

If needed, how does she know I know how
to use a sword? That old knight can probably tell,
but my skill cannot compare to his. I only studied kendo for a few years. Still, she can tell even
though I am just a novice? Those must be some
well-trained eyes. How should I respond to this

situation? Showing them all number 7,

"That sounds like an excellent plan princess, but if I could be so bold as to hear your name; yesterday's meeting was a little rushed, and we were not properly introduced." The princess gets even redder and responds with,

"Y-y-y-yes indeed, I am the first princess of the Twilight Kingdom, Releina Maya Yuno la Twilight. I hope that you will take care of me." Her maid gasps as soon as she finishes talking and the old knight raises an eyebrow. Lifting my hand to my heart and with a gentle bow, I reply,

"I am the hero Seigi, and I hope to work well together from now on Princess Releina, it would honor me to assist you in any way I can."

"Then once you are ready Mia will lead you to the dining room, Seigi-sama." The princess turns to leave and almost runs down the hall with her maid and the old knight in tow.

I have a feeling that something is not right here. Starting over with a new social structure is troublesome. From this moment forward, I will be hyper-observant of everyone around me and their interactions with one another. I have to find out what normal is here so I can find out my place before I disrupt this any further. Even if I am to be a hero here, I still don't have an actual idea of what that is and I don't want to die soon so I will need to get stronger than those demons.

This will be hard work, but it is work I am accustomed to. I will not fall behind or push too far ahead. Considering this world's history, I don't have to get rid of the demons just fulfill my job of protecting this kingdom and seeing that it keeps going long after I am gone. Completely reasonable goals so long as no calamity befalls this kingdom. Thinking reminds me of those stories again, but I am not one of those protagonists. There are many other heroes here and I am not one to die for my beliefs because I have none, I only have my personal goal of living my life as I see fit and not straying too far from that path.

Fortunately, thinking about it logically the fact that I have already had one unforeseeable act happen to me another is that much less likely to happen or does that mean it is more likely? Is that a physics question or philosophical? More things I wish I read more on. I guess I can only deal with whatever is right in front of me; planning for the future now is impossible. At least until I know more about this world. Better get started.

Anna

That hero was amazing, just like princess Releina said. I almost fainted just like she did, but my training kicked in once she fell. I am trained to cast restoration magic, my specialty, on her immediately. Releina is powering all the castle's defenses, normal sleeping is fine but if she passes out, the connection could be severed. My prime duty is to see that that never happens and if it happens, I have to help reconnect her.

Releina has a unique magic circle tattooed on to the small of her back, which focuses and allows her mana to seep into the castle from anywhere inside it. The circle looks to be a large dot on her back from even a slight distance but when I look at it closely, you can see that it is lots of little circles inside a large one. They are all kinds of sizes and overlap each other so it would look solid from even a meter away from it.

Roland said it was his masterpiece; it took all of his research into magic circles to create and even a dream or two to finally come to this design. Her mother the queen has a completely different magic circle on her back. One that had been used for generations but it seems the same one would not work for Releina since she has far more mana than her mother. It kind of weirds me out honestly, if I look at it for too long, my head gets fuzzy. One time I passed out while giving her a massage because I could not stop looking at it. Since then I always put a towel over it while washing her or during a massage.

As for seeing the hero this morning, it is lucky I came with her, normally while in the castle I don't have to stay by her side all the time. Releina prefers that I do other work and keep up with my training instead of staying with her all the time. After the morning meal, I would go to work in the nursery till lunch. Then I would stay with her for the rest of the day unless I have training. However, because of what happened yesterday, the high court mage Roland ordered me to stay by her side until we are sure that this will not happen again. Now we are quickly leaving the hero's room heading to the dining room to wait for him but.....

"No, no, no, what did I just do. How could I do that, what am I going to do now, and that response? What was that, did he agree, already? No, no, no, that cannot be, it must be that he doesn't know what I said means here." The princess is having a mental breakdown, completely unlike her.

"Princess I must tell you, that is quite a common greeting from my home country and I believe that this hero also hails from the same country. So there should not be any problem and even then I don't think it would be a problem to begin with." Sir Suzuki tries to calm the princess. However, I am sure she cannot even hear him right now.

As for me, I am still in shock with the entire event. The hero Seigi's aura was overwhelming; that pressure, it is almost the same as Releina's level of mana or even greater. However, I could tell it was under full control, unlike with Releina. He grips it tightly deep inside him. How can he already have that kind of control? Not even masters have that kind of control, I don't even know how that is possible; our training doesn't even mention how you can compress your mana like that.

Mia is not head maid for nothing, remaining calm while in the presence of that hero. How did last night go, I wonder what happened? The first maid serving new heroes is charged with calming their hearts. Meaning almost anything could have happened. There are no official records of what happens to heroes when they go through the summoning process but there are many rumors. I will have to talk to her as soon as possible. She may have already had a taste, and I know that is worrying Releina.

"To think Princess Releina would be

so bold as to propose to the Hero on his second day," I say casually turning her a bright red. This is so fun, I have not been able to tease her like this in years. Not since Eros was visiting.

"Anna, say nothing. It is bad enough that Mia heard that father and mother will know in no time. I don't want you spreading rumors too." Yup, she did not even hear Sir Suzuki's comment, not that it matters, just as she said, Mia heard everything and soon the king will know too. So it all depends on how he sees this.

We arrive at the dining hall. Normally the princess has breakfast with the royal family or with me in her room. However, the king has stated that starting today she will dine with Sir Seigi and assist him with acclimating to the kingdom. Now, why could that be I wonder?

We only have to wait a few minutes before Sir Seigi arrives with Mia, she is looking thrilled, I must talk to her alone soon. The cooks rush about serving the princess and Sir Seigi; he is looking around watching everyone's movements, that only he and the princess are eating may seem odd to him. Mia is behind Sir Seigi while Sir Suzuki and I are behind the princess both of us ate while it was still dark out, as for Mia, who knows. Their meal is simple eggs, bacon, and bread. Most heroes are fine with the meals prepared in the castle, our food is like what they had back home.

Inside the kingdom, we have farms for all kinds of fresh crops and animals thanks to the knowledge of past heroes. There is a network of large aqueducts running all over the kingdom, taking water from the mountain range to the east and the enormous lake in the south, to everywhere else. There are even magic circles set up in key places to make water if the supply runs low, and there is a desalination magic circle to make freshwater in the north. I don't know how it all works, but food and water is not a problem anywhere in the kingdom. That seems to be the key reason other human nations go to war with us, it is also the thing we trade the most outside of our nation.

Some of the newest livestock farms are in the north, a hero from before I was born, started fish farms, and farms for other sea creatures. Sir Suzuki loves eating all of those things, it seems he came from an island nation; I don't really care for fish but I love shrimp especially fried. Since we work in the castle, we can have all of those things shipped here easily. You could get them anywhere in the kingdom but they are expensive everywhere but the port cities and here in the capital. Sir Suzuki said that the new hero is from his old country, I should tell the cooks, he may like the same foods as Sir Suzuki. That seems like it is something that Releina would not care to notice; I should tell her later.

We don't have many other resources inside the kingdom, but food and water are scarce everywhere else in the world, let alone all the different kinds we have. Circles to make water are not even a secret; the church has had them for hundreds of years, every nation has them. The thing that makes the kingdom a true superpower is our mana. Because heroes marry into royalty or nobility, high mana levels are passed on. After all these many generations, the average amount of mana everyone has in the kingdom is leaps and bounds higher than people outside of it. That vast supply of mana spread all over the nation allows us to use magic circles for almost everything.

Learning those spells is hard, but funneling mana into a circle is easy. The way we use magic here is unlike anywhere else in the world because no other nation has enough mana to do these things. Let me put it into perspective. The average person in the kingdom using a water making magic circle could create enough water for themselves and their children each day. Outside of the kingdom, it would take ten to twenty people to make that same amount of water. That is not even taking into account the nobility or royalty, some of them use water magic to fight and can make tons of it easily.

Needless to say, that means that all of our soldiers are far stronger than everywhere else because they can use more magic than others. The first King set up this entire system, the "Hero King". He took many wives and had many children; all to create a power base for the future, focused on mana. So while we are not rich in natural resources, by using magic food and water, the basis for civilization is in great abundance because we have mana. That is why heroes are so important to our world not just because they are powerful and fight against the demons but because their lines give nations more mana and therefore more power in the long run.

Stealing heroes seems to be a common thing for other nations. I mean not really stealing them but enticing them. Kidnapping them would be impossible; no one born here aside from a hero's direct descendant could compare to even the weakest hero. Smaller nations live and die depending on their hero's bloodline, one small nation far from us was even started just because a noble from here left with their entire family. Just a handful of people with exorbitant amounts of mana was enough to save an entire nation in the far western lands.

I don't remember what family left or why, but it was generations ago and they have since lost a lot of their power, a shadow of who they once were. They might not even have more mana that I do since it has been several generations since they left. I know that my family is about 5 generations removed from the royal family and hero blood but we still have lots of mana. Other noble families like Mia's are only two or three generations removed and some of them are almost as strong as royals.

Releina is royalty and since many heroes have mixed with them they are almost as powerful as direct descendants. Even though it has been a few generations since a new hero married into the royal family. Not counting the one twenty years ago, but he did not have any children. The royal family's mana has not weakened in the slightest. However, with her own abnormal amount of mana you could easily mistake her for a hero. Though she cannot compare combat wise since she has almost no control of it. The complete opposite of her younger sister. Princess Lilynette has perfect control of her mana, but she has an infinitesimal fraction of the amount Releina does.

However, she has no affinity as she is a saint. She has manifested a unique saintly power. Meaning both princesses are not fit for combat and remain in the castle. The only royals fit for fighting are the two princes and if one of them lives long enough; they will be the next king. If not, the more likely thing would be that Releina would be queen, though according to her that is not a possibility. She said if it comes to it Lilynette should be old enough by then to take the crown and she can be left to her own devices.

Oh my, all these things running through my head because Releina just had to go over everything last night. I did not know even half of these things yesterday, but the two of us stayed up almost all night going over all kinds of documents. Having to use restoration magic in place of sleep is not good for you, but I guess once in a while should be fine. All the ministers gave me everything they could once they heard that Releina wanted them.

Some of those old people are terrified of her for some incomprehensible reason. Her father only limited the information she could access about magic. There was an order from the queen that went out to all the ministers, about an hour, before I went to gather the information. That ordered them to give Releina anything she wanted to study regardless of secrecy.

Seems like the queen is still holding on to her dream of having Releina take over after the king retires. The King holds all the power officially but I know that the two of them make all the important decisions together; the queen is his most trusted advisor. She would likely be the true ruler if she had not married into the royal family; just like the king's mother was the one that ruled before he took over from her in her old age.

Releina gets through breakfast without breaking down, so I think that is a win for her. Next, she and the hero have a lecture with Roland about magic. Most people only get training in the element they are attuned with so I don't have a good grasp of magic theory. This will be enlightening for me. I will have to stay with her in case of another incident, but I should be able to just spend my day observing these two. This will be fun. Seeing Releina acting so out of the ordinary is a marvellous feeling, I did not believe she would ever act like this again, not since her cousin left the kingdom.

Seigi

Breakfast went well enough, only the princess and I ate. It seems they are already treating me differently from normal heroes. This level of "uniqueness" is still fine, but I have to be careful about how they are viewing me while I still do not have a solid grasp of their culture. Next, we are going to our magic lesson. I will have to be extra careful to only show what is to be expected of me.

Perhaps even less. Then I can make up for it in sword training. It is possible that I am far stronger here than back home. My body certainly feels lighter. That feeling of increased ease of motion makes me wonder about the gravity here even more, and Suzuki said that he would handle my training personally so I guess I should be stronger than normal people. After she finishes her meal, the princess rises and states.

"Hero Seigi-sama, I will now show you to the high court mage's chamber for our lesson in magic theory and practical application. You will not be training in using magic until we have determined what element you are attuned with and you have a better grasp on how magic works here." I reply to her and use number 2.

"Very well Releina-hime please lead the way."

"H-h-hime." The princess stutters. Oh, that did not translate. Some Japanese terms must have integrated into their culture so they are not translated like everything else. I will have to be wary of this in the future.

"Princess Releina, that is the common way for people from our land to speak to a princess." Suzuki tries to calm her with some of our common knowledge, but it doesn't look like she heard him. She is blushing again when Mia interrupts.

"Seigi-sama if you would follow me," She gestures to follow her and leads us down a different hall heading deeper into the castle. The princess and her entourage follow us.

If I had to guess what I said means here, hime is likely a term of endearment for one's beloved, like saying my darling. Referring to someone as a princess with the hime honorific here seems to show closeness and attachment. I don't think this problem can get worse, so it's fine just leaving it.

Mia is leading us some distance from the dining room to another enormous door. This one is rather plain looking. It is large, not ornate. Mia then immediately pushes open the door. Maybe they just don't knock on doors here. Though within the castle could be some kind of exception, if the need arises I will most likely still knock but I will keep a mental note of this.

All of us enter. The air here is moldy and smells of old books. Along the walls are enormous bookcases full of books of all sizes and covers in many colors and scrolls and wooden planks. There is a metal gate in the far back of the room, it's obviously a restricted section. That old man from yesterday is sitting at a large round table in the center of the room.

He has several books open near him and one with a black cover and a gold chain around it in his arms. The book in his arms has the title "New Moon" and "Death Magic". It is likely from that locked up area in the back of the library. Seems they are giving me some dangerous information right off the bat. I have to memorize everything he tells me today.

"Ah, Seigi-sama and Princess Releina, you both are early risers I see. I have been reading here waiting for you both. Please take a seat anywhere, I will begin the lecture once you're seated." There are only two chairs open here and Suzuki pulls one of them out for the princess and then Mia pulls the other one out and offers it to me. I don't like the way I am being treated differently from Suzuki, but it is likely because of an assumed position I will have in the kingdom, eventually. They are likely preparing for me to lead people in future war efforts considering I am far younger than Suzuki. Meaning I will have a higher position than a bodyguard or they are already planning on setting me up with the princess, most likely both. The two of us take our seats and Roland begins,

"Magic is a phenomenon that occurs when something uses mana. It can be divided into 8 base elements and a color that is associated with them: fire is red, water is blue, lightning is yellow, ice is purple, earth is orange, wind is green, holy is white, and, death is black." He paused longer than before with that last one. Death is naturally feared by humans, I guess death magic is equally feared.

"Huh... Oh never mind just thinking," The princess breaks his lecture with an odd comment. Judging by her face, I think she has never heard of death magic before now. It might be a taboo subject. Which would explain why it's in a bound book.

"Ok then, we can use all elements in three distinct ways: self augmentation commonly called strengthening magic, detrimental augmentation called weakening magic, and elemental manipulation. Each element does each of these different, but most people only use strengthening or elemental manipulation. Strengthening and weakening use less mana so outside of the kingdom that is normally the only magic normal people use. Elemental manipulation uses lots of mana and is the hardest type of spell to cast. In the kingdom, anyone that uses elemental manipulation as their primary offense weapon is considered a mage and have said title. All soldiers in the army can use magic, but every one that is not a mage only strengthens themselves before entering combat. Now onto the elements.

Fire can increase one's strength and releases heat that can damage anything around the user. It can also place burns on an opponent that will sap their strength, or create fire and use it as a weapon. The last one, elemental manipulation has no set use, with fire as the example one can throw fireballs, fire arrows, fire axes, even fire cats. Power and shape are not universal. Everyone is encouraged to find what image works for them. If you force yourself to create a form that you are not familiar with, it will be weaker and take more mana to make.

Another thing, strengthening and weakening can only be placed on living things. If you go around trying to place one on an inanimate object, it will either fail or miss fire as elemental manipulation but with a weaker effect. Magic circles can be used to assist in casting all types of magic, though most magic circles are family secrets. Nobles have them etched into their armor and weapons to aid them in battle.

A sword might have a fireball spell on its hilt so one can unleash it right after a strike or one's armor has strengthening circles inside it to allow you to easily cast the spell right before the battle begins. Shields have detrimental circles on them to cast weakening on enemies that attack you. Helms have holy circles that subdue fear in them. If I remember correctly one noble family even has healing circles in all their armor to assist healers in healing family members wounded in battle.

Now as for water, it can raise one's strength and defense, reduce enemies' speed and strength, or manipulate existing water to use as a weapon. If the person has enough mana and the right attunement, they can even create water."

"Question!" I interrupt this time.

"Fire can augment strength but water can do both strength and defense; does fire increase strength more than water does?"

"A fine question, now as for the answer," Ro-

87

land gazes quizzically into the air as he ponders how to answer my question.

"We don't know.   Each person's mana changes effectiveness based on their own mana's strength, how much mana they are using, and their natural affinity. Most people can only use one or two elements and focus on whichever is stronger for them. Theoretically, there are differences, like you said, in how each element augments a user. However, there is no way to standardize it. Even using magic circles to remove a user's will from the equation, spells will vary in effectiveness based on the person's mana that is casting the spell." This seems very troubling. It will be difficult to level off any magic I can use. Perhaps I should refrain from trying out magic in front of people for a bit.

"Ok back to the elements, lightning can enhance speed and strength, weaken enemy strength and defense or generate electricity. This magic is generally seen as the weakest in elemental manipulation. It is hard to shape and control in battle and most armor will redirect it into the ground, users of this magic only use strengthening or another element in which they are proficient. Though heroes that use lighting don't share this sentiment, they use lightning easily and it ways others could never hope to emulate.

The ice element enhances defense but also slows down the user, it will also lower an opponent's speed and strength. Using it to generate cold or change water into ice are the basics of elemental manipulation, but if one's mana is powerful enough, this magic can kill the easiest. As you know a human's body is mostly water and if one's mana is of greater quality than another's, you can overcome a person's natural resistance to magic and freeze them. Even only freezing partially can be fatal. There are only two recorded people in our history that could do this. First, a hero whose unique magic was ice and would freeze demons solid even from a distance, and second was their child who could freeze part of an enemy with just a touch, both never fell in battle."

He emphasized this story and was even smiling the entire time while talking about ice magic. This must be the level they are expecting of me. I will take that into consideration, magic that appears to instant kill is very strong and heroes seem to be able to do it from a distance. That is a good benchmark.

"Earth magic increases strength and normally lowers speed. However, there are exceptions to the latter. It sometimes makes enemies heavier, with the varying effect of just slowing an enemy or crushing them to death. The latter being extremely rare, even for heroes. This seems to depend on the difference in the quality of mana instead of overcoming resistance. There seem to be many variables that can change the effectiveness of the weakening. So even if a hero can crush one enemy, another may simply be slowed down. This makes it very useful against weak opponents but inversely bad against strong ones, regardless of one's own strength. Elemental manipulation of the earth is not as offensive as it is defensive. Creating things out of the earth or moving it around is rather slow, but earth generated by magic is very rich in minerals and is used for all crops.

Wind can raise strength, defense, and speed. As for weakening, the range is wide from doing nothing at all to suffocation of an enemy; the latter doesn't deal with magic resistance like before but instead takes a long time to take effect. Wind users use elemental manipulation as this is the element that doing so is the easiest. The most skilled users can use strengthening spells and elemental manipulation while fighting.

Holy magic only heals the living or removes detrimental effects like fear. Strengthening and weakening terminology doesn't apply to holy magic; its primary use is most commonly either healing one's self or another. However, when used on demons or undead holy magic will, regardless of the user's will, damage or destroy them to varying degrees. This effect can be heightened by instead of casting a healing spell attempting the use of elemental manipulation to make light weapons and attack said demon or undead. Meaning that holy element cannot hurt the living at all so even though it is strong against demons, holy users are healers."

Roland paused for some time after finishing. He takes a glass of water from behind him, drinks it all and puts it behind himself. Then he breathes deeply and slowly for a few minutes. Everyone pays it no mind, so I wait along with them. After a lengthy pause, he continues.

"Now then, death magic, there are only two recorded users in all of our history, both demon lords and the only known effect is causing instant death to many people over a wide area. The Demon Lord of the New Moon, the oldest and most powerful demon lord. That demon lord supposedly has never been confirmed killed, but has not been seen since his fight with the first hero 'The Hero King.' That demon lord killed countless people and demons with his black mist. There were even rumors that he could kill magic. Fifty years after the first hero was summoned and saved this nation he fought the Demon Lord of the New Moon with two other heroes.

While protecting the other two from the

black mist he dealt a powerful blow to the demon lord, by leaping into a cloud of black mist, shocking both enemies and allies he created an opening from which to strike that demon lord. They assumed the demon lord did not die from the attack and simply fled, but even if he fell, he would revive later so the specifics do not matter.

The second has some conflicting reports, but a powerful demon thought to be a demon lord unleashed black mist during a war around sixty years after the Demon Lord of the New Moon disappeared. This was within one of the southernmost nations. Reports said there were only a few survivors, and they all went mad. Since the second incident did not happen to us and with such shaky reports, we consider it a half-truth. There was most likely a demon lord at that battle and his magic could have been death magic, but even if we take those as facts there is not enough information to use in any kind of meaningful way. Aside from a historical perspective.

We believe that a person's heart has sway over a person's magic and while demons hate humanity, they still have some feelings for their own kind. Yet, The Demon Lord of the New Moon was known to kill both humans and demons alike with his magic. The fact that no other known demon has shown that magic or that disregard for even their own kind lead magic researchers to tie those facts together. Death magic can only be used by a being that looks down on and doesn't recognize other life as meaningful, truly horrific magic.

Now then, having said that, no one has seen that demon lord ever since. However, it is the most dangerous existence in our history and the King felt it necessary to inform you about all potential threats to our Kingdom. Most heroes are never told this story officially, I am sure Sir Suzuki has heard about it several times in passing as it is a well-known story in the general populous. I am telling you this now because of the king's order and it directly connects to your magic lecture." Just then a bell rings from behind the old man.

"Oh my, this late already, I have my normal duties to attend to Sir Seigi. We can continue tomorrow. I have heard Princess Releina has prepared notes on the more pertinent problems our kingdom faces. I shall leave you two to it, I must be going." Roland stands up and heads out of the room. The princess has a sullen face.

"Before we go over the notes, I would like to have a word with Seigi-sama alone." She says this while looking at Mia.

The princess must not be able to give her a direct order, or is she just being polite? Either way, this proves Mia is not a normal maid, she must have some kind of seniority. Maybe Mia was there to watch me and determine if I was a danger or not? I had thought her observing me was just for normal reasons. Though I have been my model self for over 5 years, that little hiccup when I was summoned has been the only time "it" has fallen since I decided to put it on. If anything, her watching me should help ease any potential fears anyone might have. Ok, great, I should be well on my way to fitting in here, I just need some more baseline information.

"All right princess, we will be just on the other side of the door. Call us once you are done," Mia responds with an amiable brief smile. Mia, the princess's maid, and Suzuki leave the room. I wonder what the princess wants to talk about? Once the door closes, Releina begins.

"Seigi-sama I wish to discuss the details of your summoning." Interesting, not at all what I was expecting. Was it that different from normal?

"Normally the summoning circle, once filled with mana, changes color to correspond with one element. This color tends to be the hero's unique magic. Ah yes, the hero's unique magic is a misnomer, it follows all the same rules as everyone's magic, it is just beyond them. No normal person's magic can compare to a hero's.

Your summoning was different." She told me everything that she saw that day from just before the ritual to when she fainted, trying to play that off as mana exhaustion. So every color was shown and then it ended with black, what does this mean?

"Sir Suzuki had mentioned that you might be proficient in several elements which would be unprecedented, but no hero has ever had 'Death Magic' before either. A person's magic comes from their heart. We believe it to reflect their soul, of course, that is not a fact just what we believe." Releina looks sullen after that remark.

"Not to say anything bad about you Seigi-sama even if you have that magic. I don't think that kind of connection can be even considered. But after hearing that story of the first hero, my great ancestor the 'Hero King' I felt I needed to tell you." This is some troublesome news, I maintained number 2 throughout the conversation, not wanting to have any kind of response to this news.

In the back of my mind, I consider all kinds of potential lines. I need to figure out my magic by myself before I can decide how I can fit in. I will have to show off in my sword training today since I cannot make any headway in magic until I know more about myself and death magic. Releina called the others back, and we began going over her notes on the kingdom. But I am only half listening while determining my plan and mentally going over my old sword training.

Suzuki The White Knight

Crash, crack, snap. The wooden training sword shatters after three hits. I am training the new hero, Seigi, in swordsmanship. I thought he had some training and was right; though it seems it is just some basics. The broken sword is mine, Seigi isn't used to his strength but is adjusting to it quickly. This is the third sword he has destroyed. I was right to do his training myself. His first attack shattered my sword and almost tore my arm off.

Seigi was far faster than I expected, but I could still block. Unfortunately, the training sword could not stand up and shattered instantly; I blocked with my other arm instinctually. Seigi immediately knew he put too much power into the strike and tried to pull back, but he still hit my arm. If it was anyone else that would have ended their fighting career even with healing magic, tearing muscles and shattering bone like that doesn't heal right. Luckily my body returns to normal after a few moments of me focusing on healing, I don't even have to focus that makes it go a little faster.

After Seigi has a good hold of his body, I can let him train against normal soldiers. Surprisingly enough, he is training in the same suit he came here with. He told me it was better than any armor we might have. It not hindering his movements sold me. I cannot imagine what kind of technology was used to make it, but I assume it is like bulletproof vests.

We clash again, one, two, three, four. The swords groan in protest but don't break and Seigi smirks like he finally figured it out for himself. Now I can push him to see how skilled he is. Our sparring lasts for some time, the princess and maids have been watching the entire time but now we seem to have drawn a crowd. The sides of the courtyard have palace guards and maids from every division watching. They are even filling the windows; I catch a few nobles watching intently. The red knight passes by once but does not stay and now the king has shown up in one of the highest windows; he is watching his daughter and our match.

The sound of our sword clashing is likely echoing through the castle halls. I am using my full strength however it is obvious to anyone that Seigi is holding back tremendously. His mana is not fluctuating in the slightest. He easily makes up for his lack of technique with keen judgements and raw speed. Carefully watching each of my strikes unfold before readying his counter. Unfortunately, there is no way I can tell if this power of his is augmented by mana or not. Unable to successfully parry an attack, I meet it with a counter, both of our swords crack and break apart.

"Sir Seigi, I think this is enough for today. I feel I have a good measure of your skill and strength with that match. You still have much to learn; during the latter half you were making up the difference of skill with sheer speed. Given time, you will easily surpass me." His skills are just above a novice, but his strength and speed are likely beyond measure. He might be faster than the Hero Cesar and he is far stronger than the Crimson Slayer, even if he cannot use magic he will be a great boon to the war effort.

"Yes, while not as refined as the white knight your movements were fluid, not a wasted move from what I could see." The princess remarks. I am surprised she could see all of that. Not once did she take her eyes off of him while we were sparring.

"Ever since arriving I have felt lighter walking normally has been a little difficult. With this, I feel like I finally got a good grip on my body again. However, it seems like we made quite a spectacle of ourselves." Seigi makes an awkward smile while looking at the crowd that has gathered.

All the young guards look to be inspired

99

and many of the maids seem quite taken with him. Strength is the most important quality people look for here; it makes sense everyone would be drawn to him; he is easily the strongest hero I have ever seen. Physically at least, Mikeal's magic is perfect for eliminating entire armies and many other heroes were the same as him in the kingdom's history.

Those kinds of heroes did well against the demon armies, but fell once they had to fight the demon lords. That is it, Seigi's strength reminds me of the demon lord to the east, enough power to level mountains. I wonder how the war with the demons will go with a hero comparable to the demon lords. Even if fighting armies doesn't suit him; if he can take a demon lord alone, how will they react?

"All right enough gawking everyone back to work!" With a loud clap, a man disperses the crowd and approaches Seigi and I.

Jin Aranwell, a powerful young noble from the south, not an unpleasant man but I cannot get along with him ever since he became the patron of the red knight. Long ago he was one of the men that wanted princess Releina's hand, but that ended quickly enough. Like most young nobles he has an irrational fear of the princess, they all seem to fear her almost instinctively. The way prey fears large predators, the difference in mana makes her seem like an imposing thing to them, instead of just a young girl. A condition that doesn't afflict Sir Seigi.

"I am sure if this was a genuine match that strength you showed at the beginning would have made an enormous difference, and all that was without using any magic. We can have you start with actual swords and armor against the guards and other knights starting tomorrow." Jin comments. He stopped farther away from Seigi than I am but has positioned himself farthest from the princess.

"So you have been watching since the beginning Sir Jin," I ask him, taking great care to look him in the eye.

"How could I not, after hearing all those rumors of the new hero? Please let me introduce myself, I am Jin Aranwell, Archduke of the central southern territories." He addresses Seigi in a respectful tone. He must want to bring him into his sphere of influence.

Too bad for him the king already has plans for Seigi, if all goes well he will be wed to the princess within the year. He should also take Anna and a few others as well if the princess permits. The last few heroes have sired no children. The blue knight has problems similar to mine but not truly the same, and Mikeal might be sterile. He has had many women unofficially, but none of them have ever conceived.

Heroes' secondary duty is to pass down their genes to the next generation to increase the kingdom's power. Most heroes have had many wives and mistresses for that very reason. These last few summonings have been a problem. No new blood has been added to the royal family or the nobility. Even if Releina doesn't become queen, her children may take the crown in the next generation if they are Seigi's children.

Having royal blood and being a hero's direct descendant would immediately put them higher on the succession list. That tradition was set to always ensure the best future possible at the expense of the present. The crowd has now dispersed so we have no more unwanted viewers; after everyone else is gone Seigi continues the conversation with Sir Jin.

"I am the new hero Seigi." Raising his right arm to his chest the same way he introduced himself to the king.

"I would love to have you spar with my guard at some point when you have the time," Jin responds to Seigi.

"It would be fine with me but my training is being run by Sir Suzuki you would have to go through him to set that up."

"We can have that done on whatever day you wish Sir Jin, Sir Seigi will train around this time for a few days before resting and continuing for another few days." Even if he wants to keep his training going you have to let your body rest and rebuild.

"That is a very rushed schedule, is it not? A new hero tends to have a few weeks of rest and acclimation before going so earnestly into training." Jin seems puzzled, but that is to be expected this is a change from the norm, but the king wants to see how strong Seigi is as soon as possible. If Seigi had objected or looked unwell, I would have slowed things down, but he was perfectly willing to the point of eagerness for his training to begin.

"Honestly, I would not know what to do with myself if I was to just stay in my room acclimating. I am grateful to get out and have a good workout. I have always been the type to keep moving, especially when things get hard." Seigi responds with a smile that makes even Jin blush.

"I can understand that way of thinking, not everyone is the same, I look forward to seeing your continued training. Maybe we can have a match as well, not that I would have a chance. But I would like to see how I measure up. Perhaps next week we can have our training session. I only have a few more weeks in the capital before I must return home. I will have my secretary submit a proper request to you, Sir Suzuki, I will see you later. Princess Releina, good evening to you." Jin leaves us and our group is the only one left in the courtyard.

"Princess, it is getting late. We should head to the dining room and then let Sir Seigi take all of this in. There is no need to rush things on the first day." I believe today has been a splendid start and judging by how quickly the castle staff and Jin reacted, the rumor mill has been working overtime.

"Yes, that sounds great. Seigi-sama, any objections?" Princess Releina is getting far more proactive.

"No, nothing wrong with that, today has been very enlightening." Once again he smiles at the princess and she tumbles to the ground. Anna rushes over to her; Sir Seigi seems to be embarrassed this keeps happening. I wonder how long she will be like this?

Seigi

After dinner, I return to my room with Mia. At the door, I turn to her and ask.

"If possible, I would like to be alone tonight." I need to check many things without her prying eyes.

"Normally I would be required to stay with you, but the king has given me discretionary permission regarding you Seigi-sama. If you are fine with me staying outside the door, then it should be fine." She really is under orders to watch my every move. Is that because they are wary of me or worried about me? Logically both, but this entire world doesn't seem to follow the logic I knew before.

"I hate to put you out but I need to be alone tonight, thank you." I show her number 5 and close the door. This is no time to be worried about those kinds of problems.

While closing the door I hear a small gasp from the other side of the door. As I thought the door is not soundproof, she is staying just outside the door. That she was in my room all night last night likely means they don't have some kind of listening device or magic that is monitoring me. In any case, I do a once over the room to check for cracks or peepholes, anything that would let someone spy on me. After finding nothing of the sort, I take a seat on the floor in the middle of the room.

I don't know how long they will have her stay with me and asking her to stay out several times in a row will be a little awkward. So I need to get this done as quickly as possible or it will start some rumors. They told me magic comes from the heart. I wonder if they meant figuratively or literally? If they meant it literally than it most likely has something to do with this unnatural warmth I have felt since getting here. My first thought was that it is the reason for me feeling so light and stronger here, not that it cannot be both. However, it is the only thing I have noticed that feels different from before.

Let us begin. After getting into the lotus position, I meditate. As soon as I cut off external stimuli, I feel it more clearly, the warmth, it grows exceeding the confines of my heart and fills my entire body. Instantly my body feels stronger and lighter than before, but I am short of breath and feel fatigued like nothing I have felt since coming here. A moment later and my skin is burning, the warmth has become an intense heat and is trying to escape from my body. Through the growing pain, I fight for control. After an intense struggle that lasted for what seemed like forever, I forced it back into my heart.

It takes a moment longer to control my breathing. I would like to rest, but I need to get as much done tonight as possible. I opened my eyes to tell what time it is, it's still pitch black outside, it seems I still have some time. There is also some dim light and a slight shadow outside my room. It seems like she is not sleeping tonight. I bet normally she is meant to keep me 'company' while observing me. They have been doing this for a very long time. It would make sense that there would be some kind of procedure to welcome their heroes. Normal people would struggle to accept this odd situation. The maids are likely trained on how to help them adjust as well as get them to want to help the kingdom.

Missing sleep for a night should not be a problem, even with that exhausting experience just now. I have done it many times before back home. Two or three days without sleep can be dangerous, but one won't be a problem. Closing my eyes again I focus on the warmth, I try calmly letting it out slowly. It's trying to expand beyond my heart like before, it feels like a balloon ready to burst. I need to focus on it. Maybe I should have it flow along my veins, perhaps giving some visualization to it will allow for more control. Though

I don't want it going everywhere, that will only lead to the same as last time, maybe just slower.

If this is mana, then I need to release it from my body, but in a small enough way that the reaction from earlier doesn't happen. So a minor part of myself that I can control easily. Yes, I will have it flow to my fingertips. After deciding that, I redirect the flow along my arm to my fingertips and I feel the warmth flowing through and stopping at my fingers, filling them. I try to hold it back from building up and filling my entire arm, but it is still flowing from my heart along my veins to my hand. It feels hotter, but it is not painful. It seeps out of my hand. Even as it leaves my body, I can still feel it and control it. This must be magic.

While maintaining the flow of the warmth just leaving my hand, not getting too big or too far from me, I open my eyes. The sight I am greeted by is a pure black mist slowly rising from my hand. I close my eyes, stop the flow from leaking out of my hand, and try to think. Dammit, of course, I just knew it. Does this mean those people were right about me back then? No, I have lived my life since then knowing they were wrong, the fact that I had gotten so far proves that. I had to change schools to restart my life, that kind of option is not available here, I cannot make the same mistake.

No one can ever see this.

Once I resolve myself, I force it all back into my heart. In this world of magic and swords, I will seal my magic away and put my all into my sword training. They are not right, I will live a normal life with just the right amount of uniqueness and fulfill my role in this world. My name is Seigi and I am a 'Hero'.

When I opened my eyes again, it was still dark, but not as much as before. I guess I will at least rest my body till morning. After standing up, I get into bed wide awake and wait for dawn with the resolve I have had for years to live my life free of those shackles. My place has already been decided I will not lose it again and anyone that gets in my way will be eliminated without the slightest hesitation regardless of who it may be.

It has been a week since I decided to permanently seal my magic. My days have homogenized. I get up at dawn with a greeting by Mia. She is still staying in my room, I only had one other night without her since I determined my magic affinity. Never once have I seen her eat or sleep but she is the head maid so that kind of skill is not completely out of bounds in a world with magic.

However, the way she looks at me has

changed ever so slightly. It happened after I showed her number 5, as I feared it would, but I had to ensure she would not intrude on me that night. Aside from the way she looks at me, there have been no unprofessional actions from her so I should not have much to worry about.

After breakfast I have magic lessons with Princess Releina, I have made no progress using magic and the princess cannot use it for other reasons. It has continued to be just lectures from Roland on theory and practical application for commercial and wartime use. He also does demonstrations of magic circles and various strengthening effects in the courtyard with some guards and maids. The fact that every element is tied to a color has significance in battle. Soldiers can see the aura around each other to determine the type of strengthening a person has and the size of the aura also shows you how strong an opponent is allowing you to act accordingly.

Building this skill to make a proper judgment is what military training focuses on, know yourself and your opponent as you will. This 'sight' is a common ability for people of this world, heroes develop it quickly, unfortunately, I have yet to gain this skill. My vision is better than back home but I can only see magic that is being used; not the aura created by strengthening effects.

There are levels of this magical sight that can even allow someone to see a person's mana inside their body, which can give you a clear edge in battle. Knowing what your opponent can do before they do it is an advantage that can be lethal. There is even a legendary form of magic sight called "Crystal Eyes"; having these eyes lets you even see the shape of one's soul and according to myth allows you to reshape it. The kingdom doesn't have anyone known in its borders that even has the weaker version of these eyes that lets them see the aura without using magic. This type of eye creates a problem for me. If people can see the darkness of my mana, they would likely be terrified. I am already hyper-vigilant of people giving me odd glances, so monitoring this should not pose a problem.

In the afternoon I go over reports from all over the kingdom with the princess; ranging from crop yields, crime rates, and foreign affairs. Crime here is a bit odd, there are almost no murders but brawling in the streets is extremely common. There is also almost no youth crime, even with a lot of orphans because of the near-constant war. They put orphans under the care of the city mayor or village elder and begin training for a future in the military. The most common crime in the kingdom is the smuggling of forbidden goods; dangerous performance-enhancing drugs into the kingdom, food out of the kingdom, and slaves into the kingdom.

The kingdom outlawed slavery hundreds of years ago, but the rest of the world is only now getting rid of the practice thanks to the work of another powerful nation far to the west. There are laws for bringing slaves into the kingdom legally, all of which require the freeing of said slave. In fact, it is common for nobles to bring slaves from other countries here to be freed and then adopt them or have them marry into their own families. This practice seems to have been created to bring fresh blood into the kingdom and collect talented individuals.

This law has obvious potential for abuse, especially since slaves that were brought into the kingdom fall under the care of the noble family that brought them here. Princess Releina commented that one noble house that had been all but wiped out during a war rose back to power after a single generation. By bringing many female slaves here and having many children of great renown born from them.

Food is so plentiful here that farmers can sell extra for higher profits outside the kingdom. Logically, merchants would jump on this opportunity. There is plenty of legal trade for them but the crown caps what it allows to be sold to foreign bodies. This seems to have been done to control the black market, with the kingdom's foods being the bulk of products on both the legal and illegal markets. The crown could affect both easily if it so desired. As for the drugs, there are many illegal in the kingdom that can strengthen and or replenishment mana.

However, healing drugs don't exist in this world, so some questionable drugs that fake healing are in the illegal category. None of these drugs are magic. They all affect the body as any drug would with chemical responses. Nobles that are on the weak side or even commoners want these drugs to increase their power while fighting, but the reason they are illegal is that they have terrible side effects.

After lessons with the princess, I have combat training with the palace guards and Sir Suzuki. By now I have fought and beaten all the guards, though I hold back not only to not wound them but also preserve their pride. A few days ago while training, a guard tried using their favorite weapon, a halberd, instead of the normal training swords. I still won, but that gave me the idea of not limiting myself to only the sword.

Since then I have been training with every kind of weapon in the palace and have encouraged the guards to experiment for themselves or to use their favorite weapons while training. With all this training, I have been able to completely control my strength and speed. However, I have not been able to push myself, and find out what the true limits of my strengths are.

That brings us to today, I am having training matches with the personal guards of Jin Aranwell, the visiting noble from the south. The princess and maids are watching from the edge of the courtyard. Releina always has a notable smile during training; her maid, who I found out was named Anna, also looks very excited while watching our training sessions. Only Mia shows no emotion.

None of his guards are noteworthy in either strength or skill, but the leader Joffrey, a lesser noble, continues to fight a losing battle for quite a while, his stamina is well above average. I wonder if he was using magic or is just naturally that resilient? All the soldiers use their strengthening magic while training against me, the only magic not allowed is elemental manipulation. Though I don't think any of these soldiers are mages, so they might not even be able to use that kind of magic.

"This was to be expected, my men would have no chance against a hero, even if you have not yet learned magic," Jin said in a slightly provocative tone. Is he trying to provoke me, insult me, or just trying to gauge my reaction to that?

"Everyone learns at their own pace, Sir Jin." The princess seems to have taken that comment negatively and rebukes him.

"I meant no disrespect, Princess Releina. I was simply stating that Sir Seigi handled them so well without magical enhancements. So once he has mastered magic, there is no telling how strong he will be. Similar to the Red Knight who slew that Demon Lord that took your uncle from us last year." That didn't sound sincere, and it seems to have angered the princess even more. I know. I can use this to learn about magic's more practical uses.

"Sir Jin how about that match you had asked for; you can even use magic to make things more interesting." Everyone falls silent.

"I think I will take you up on that offer Sir Seigi this could be my only chance to ever beat a hero in combat." His smug face shows that he really thinks he can beat me, so he must be a rather powerful combat mage. The princess runs up to me.

"Are you sure about this Seigi-sama, Sir Jin is a powerful wind magic user, his speed is matched only by the crimson slayer, and he has powerful elemental manipulation magic." Wind magic, that was the weakest element, so I think I could figure out a nice floor for magic in this world.

"Don't worry princess Releina, I need to train against people when they are using magic and the stronger the better." I try to reassure the princess, then Sir Suzuki steps forward.

"You need not worry princess, against Sir Jin, Sir Seigi can use his power to its fullest." That vote of confidence comes from Suzuki's theory about my apparent lack of magic. During one of our lectures he commented on the sense he had that my mana seems to be trapped within me and might augment me physically similar to strengthening magic but instead with pure mana.

"You hear that Princess, Sir Suzuki believes in me, but just to be sure I will use a sword, the weapon I am most comfortable with." I show her number 7 to calm her.

"If you are sure then I will believe in you, Seigi-sama." Everyone clears the courtyard, then I notice a figure in red armor in one window behind Jin. I have only seen him twice before, he never stays to watch my training like everyone else; it seems like he will watch this time. He must have been able to tell I was holding back during all the other training.

"Whenever you are ready, Sir Jin," I get into a fighting stance and wait for him to make the first move.

"Oh wind, engulf me." Jin chants and becomes surrounded by spinning green light that fades away. Chants are unnecessary for magic to work, but they help most people focus. The red and white knights are known for not chanting.

Jin prepares to dash forward, then disappears. My sword moves and I block to the right. His stance gave him away, I did not see a single movement after he took his stance. His attack lacked weight. Can he not translate his speed into striking power or is he holding back? Magic is very strange. He looks shocked at first but disappears again, lower left this time. An eye twitch revealed his plan. His strike is heavier this time but is lacking when considering his speed, he was holding back. Jin appears and disappears around me several more times but he is no longer telegraphing an attack so I hold my stance. He keeps this up for some time, he must be trying to get me to attack him.

I'm unsure if I am moving at my top speed, barely intercepting his telegraphed attacks. Magic defies common sense. It's only been two actual attacks so far but my body is heating up similar to a long sparring match. He is looking kind of happy that I blocked him; he dashes back and to the left, is he slowing down? Jin did not disappear; I could track his movements perfectly. Is he slowing down or am I the one speeding up? He doesn't look like he will attack again, so I step in to disarm him.

In one step, I closed the distance he opened with his dash. A look of shock appears on his face, it lasts only a second then he disappears again. Is he running? I did not see any attack tells that time; he must be running. I can't find him. Is it possible to keep up that insane movement speed for prolonged periods? My body is unreasonably hot, yet it's comfortable, but I don't think I can't keep this up for too much longer.

"Oh wind, become my blade." His voice is coming from above me, he is high in the air above me, I still can't get a read on his next move.

Perhaps that must be it; magic attacks don't have similar tells like physical ones. A green light swirls around him again and it forms into wide-angle blades and they fly towards me, they are not moving fast, I can dodge them easily. So this is elemental manipulation. It looks like solid blocks of air have been fashioned into blades. Maybe I should test how resistant my suit is to magic right now and let one hit me? This is the first time I truly feel this is a fantasy world.

Thinking about it, I want to try something fantasy-like. Also, getting hit on purpose is just not an outstanding idea so I will counter not take the hit. Stepping into the attack and with all the strength I can muster, I swing down; careful to catch the flat of the wind blade. It shatters and fades. There was minimal resistance. Is wind weak to counter attacks? The second blade is too close to strike. Forcing a recovery with sheer might, I bring my blade up to parry. The air blade runs along the length of my sword, shaving away a layer of the steel as sparks fly off it.

However, its trajectory shifts as I turn my sword. Seeing this, I throw the blade back at him. It was a gamble that the wind had formed a solid mass, but while enhancement magic seems to defy physics at every turn, elemental manipulation is supposed to try to obey the law of the world. So if it was being made to follow a trajectory and cut, I assumed it needed to be more solid than normal air. The light under Jin vanishes causing him to descend faster, dodging the blade I sent back to him. The fight is over, my weapon is essentially destroyed. The first wind blade I shattered made several small but deep cuts in the sword, while the second has cleaved off the edge of my blade. As he lands, he puts his sword in the ground and raises his hands, yielding.

"I give up, it is your win Sir Seigi." I'm a little surprised, I was going to concede once he took a stance but Jin looks exhausted and takes a knee, that magic must drain him.

Looking around me, I notice the courtyard is an enormous mess. He created a sizable amount of those wind blades and blasted the whole courtyard, except for the area immediately around me. It must have been an attack meant for the battlefield, not a duel. A cheer erupts from all sides, it seems we gathered a crowd again. It looks like everyone in the castle knows whenever something big is happening around me. Could this have to do with their magic sense? How long will it take for me to develop it myself? I heard that I should develop it once I start using magic, but that will not be happening. The princess comes running up to me.

"Seigi-sama that was amazing, you were moving as fast as the archduke with his strengthening magic. And that technique to destroy and deflect the wind blades; I have seen nothing like it. At first, I was shocked when the duke unleashed that battle magic. It is normally only used against many enemies as a trump card, as it leaves you exhausted after. However, you easily dodged the blades and even countered." Releina is beaming with excitement. None of my other sparring matches could compare to this one. I still feel burning hot, but I can feel the chilling air coming from her.

"Once I saw him keeping up with my speed and not falling for any of my feints, I bet everything on that last attack. However, Sir Seigi not only crushed it but turned it against me. Never once had I thought that kind of interaction with attack spells as possible. The speed and strength needed to attack spells is unheard of and you don't even look out of breath. You must be the only one capable of such a feat. That must have taken incredible strength and speed as well as foresight.

The only thing I have ever seen that is similar was when the Red Knight's flame sword would cut through ice spells from the demon lord on the front of the last war. However, canceling magic with magic is common enough but for you to accomplish that feat with pure physical force. I am beyond impressed, Sir Seigi, you have my thanks for the chance to spar with you."

His face right now shows genuine surprise, but he is using it to hide his fear. I am quite used to people like him. Those that pretend to not be afraid of me. The only question is why? It would not make sense for him to just fear how strong I am. No, this man has a hidden reason to be afraid of me. He is not the same as the ones back home. Changing my face to number 7, I responded to his compliment.

"I have to admit, I did not know I could move that fast, you pushed me beyond my previous limits. As for stopping the attack, even if they moved freely and with impressive speed; they were solid blades not made of steel. Parrying was simply the work of avoiding its cutting edge." There is no need to keep that a secret, anyone who saw what I did could tell how it was done. Also, it doesn't seem like that was too unusual. It can be done easier with magic so no one has ever tried to do it without before.

"Yes, well, I must rest after that exchange. I will see you at a later time, Sir Seigi. Princess Releina, good evening." Jin turns to leave, his guards follow suit. The red knight in the window left once the match was over.

"Now princess, shall we head to the dining room? I feel like eating after all this." I show her number 2 as I say this, must keep up appearances as you will.

"As you wish, resting after that level of stimuli is paramount. We have a special dinner tonight. I hope you look forward to it." The princess blushes and turns away and we head off to the din-

ing room.
Jin Aranwell

Jin returns to his room inside the castle wall, not in the main building, far from the new hero and princess that he hates so much. His guards head to the barracks for all the castle guards and he enters his empty room. For an Archduke not having any maids is an oddity but the southern lands are in tatters from the last war so he could not bring them on this trip, also all maids even ones serving the archduke fall under the crown's direct command.

Serving in rotating shifts around the entire nation, they provide the crown with eyes and ears everywhere and a military force inside all nobles' homes. Some see this as a knife at their throats, but the true purpose is to foster relationships between noble families around the kingdom. Since all maids are noble's second or third daughters, this system was set up to allow easier mixing of noble families to not stagnate their lines. However, Jin has not brought any maids with him because he believes it is the former.

Once inside the room he removes his coat and shirt revealing his body full of scars and burns covered in fresh sweat. He sits down to rest as a person moves into view from the shadows in the back of his room. Without making a sound, the red knight moves closer to Jin and pulls out a chair to sit with the archduke, with a look of anger on his face.

"That hero is frighteningly strong and without awakening his magic at that, dammit! Why did this have to happen! You saw that, right? He saw through each of the initial moves but did not rely on that knowledge either. All of my feints were seen through easily and he effortlessly parried my genuine attacks."

"You telegraphed them, so that is not unexpected. He has to have some level of combat knowledge from our world unless he is just fast enough to have seen through you and react without prior knowledge." The red knight snickers as he responds.

"Yes, but heroes are not that skilled in combat right after summoning. That theory of having prior training seems even more likely now." There is fear in Jin's voice and a hint of panic.

"I guess the white knight was right, this one has had training back in our world. The thought scares me, if it's true. I think he is more likely an athlete or a martial artist than a soldier. But I doubt he has taken a life he; doesn't have the scent of blood on him. Now if he had a weapon from back home, we would be in trouble."

"Are weapons back there that strong?" Jin almost chokes on his words as he goes pale just imagining those weapons.

"Way stronger than anything here, there are bombs that can wipe nations off the map. Also, did you see his sword after the match? That thing would not last another swing from him you could have won. However, ones from back home could last forever, never rusting or breaking." The red knight looks pleased with himself, as if he would make those weapons himself.

"So if he has a sword from your home, would that have happened?" Jin looks worried but also seems to think about what to do to counter this hero.

"Not sure; he is probably stronger now than he was there, I know you can get swords that are significantly stronger than here. But wars there have not had swords as basic equipment for over a hundred years."

"And this guy fought in wars over there, no wonder he could counter my wind blade with just a sword." Jin holds his head and stares at the table again with a look of worry on his face.

"That is what the white knight thinks, we don't know if it is true. I would like it if he would join our side though, it would be great to have someone as good as me to help fight those demons." The red knight's face contorted with anger and disgust, remembering fighting demons.

While Jin's face turns to sorrow, remembering the demon's last invasion.

"I know what you mean but the king gave him the head maid, so he has already moved to keep him in the capital. Do you think you can win?" As Jin asks that question an oddly confident grin comes across the red knight's face.

"Of course, as long as he has no magic he doesn't stand a chance against me. Even if he learns it soon it won't be as strong as my flames, I have fought two wars now with my magic. A newbie like him is nothing before me, only ash. We only have to worry about his magic being water or ice so he could weaken my magic enough that he and the old guy could be a problem for me."

"Yeah that is what I am afraid of, we will have to speed up everything, get ready, two weeks maximum; that is all we can wait. I will head back home to send word to all involved parties, but we will not have our foreign allies with the new time table. So you are the most important piece, be ready. I will make that old fool of a king pay for letting my family die like that. That old fool will get what is coming to him."

"Right, right, just remember my reward." Jin looks at him with worry on his face.

"You will get plenty once I am the king. Everyone will, we just have to do this fast; a long protracted civil war would be terrible. We have to be ready to fight the demons again within five years. That is why we cannot wait, this has to go down clean." The red knight nods as he gets up from his chair. Then he leaves through some hidden door; the same as he entered.

"I will finally be able to avenge my family. Those stupid nobles who were the ones responsible for slowing down the refortification of my family's fort and villages died at the hands of demons. But that damn king could have pushed it through easily. He is just too old and soft. Never have we had a king this old and decrepit. He should have gone to the crystal long ago. If I had taken the princess's hand I would have been able to force him out but she.

That woman is a monster, that is right, I am doing this for the kingdom. Those royals need to die, I will preserve their bloodline with the saint. No need to be angering actual gods. Yes, yes, we have to hurry before he, before Seigi, is able to stop us. This coup needs to be wrapped up with as little bloodshed as possible." Jin moves over to his cupboard and takes out a glass and bottle of wine. He sits back down and drinks slowly, trying to envision a future where he has already won.

Releina

My older brothers have returned from their posts at the border fortresses after years of being away touring our borders with demon territory. The day we summoned Seigi-sama, father declared it was too dangerous for the Royals to be on the front lines. One's work can't simply be halted immediately. So they each spent a few days ensuring the forts would run without their presence.

Having been given those forts to prove their value as king candidates, there was a need to bring in capable leaders as the capable ones before had been reorganized to not overshadow them. It seems father wants them to redeploy depending on what kind of danger is looming, until then they will be here at the castle until further notice. He also wants them to test their new strength and skills against Sir Suzuki.

This is the first dinner with the entire royal family present since little Lilynette was born. To think I had once missed the presence of my brothers, but now I can only think of them as an annoyance. As is proper, I am seated across from Seigi-sama. It would be inappropriate for a lady to sit by his side, apparently. Instead, the two of them are seated by his side. Completely monopolizing his time, they are talking about his duel with the Archduke and the situation at the border. I've only been able to share reports with Seigi-sama, so it's all second or third-hand information. The two of them have first-hand experience and Alphonse, my eldest brother, has even fought demons, though they were only scouts that appear randomly.

Father and Mother had an understanding that had allowed me to monopolize Seigi-sama during dinner. But these two just cannot seem to leave him alone. I would ask Seigi-sama a question about our magic lessons and then discuss all the day's events. Oh, how I love the look of his eyes as he recounts the day's activities. The way he stares directly into my soul, trying to discern the deepest detail and intent of my question sends shivers down my spine.

Our first family dinner, without my brothers, was a bit concerning. The way Seigi-sama knelt down to eye level and spoke with such gentleness to Lilynette sent my heart fluttering most unpleasantly. It was a needless worry. As a gentleman, Seigi-sama knows that children frighten easily by the rough nature of soldiers, so he is gentler with them than others. The children in the nursery also seem to easily take with him, he has only been there twice but all the children already love him.

Although Lilynette can't properly see his greatness. She hid behind mother the first time they met. It was likely because of her unique gift and her childishness. Like mother and I, Lilynette has an impressive amount of mana, compared to normal people. However, unlike myself or mother, her mana has manifested as a skill. She is a saint with prophetic visions. Most prophets receive divine oracles, where they predict the future. The church has many documented cases in its extensive history. However, Lilynette is special even among recorded prophets.

The exact nature of her skill isn't well understood, but she can smell someone's core and destiny. Because of this, she gets along with people quickly and those she doesn't are usually removed. She helped expose a rather significant slave trade in the capital recently. She was young and didn't understand her power. She simply said they smelled gross. Further investigations revealed a slave trade network. She also predicted the untimely death of several maids and guards.

Lilynette has started to understand her power, though she still has trouble communicating. On their first meeting, she fled from Seigisama and told mother he smelled of danger. Father had expected this. It seems everyone is certain that some kind of danger is on the horizon.

That is why my brothers were called back; to help prepare for whatever it ends up being. Lilynette once said the red knight smelled dangerous. It makes me angry that her description of them is so similar but I know despite being young she chooses her words and wording carefully. Someone being dangerous is not the same as danger following them or being surrounded by danger.

Saint's powers are linked to and thought to be the blessing of one of "The Three." Old gods that are the foundation of everything that exists and all that doesn't. Gods so old that to pray to them is in insult, only gods can pray to those great old ones. The church of the seven told my family that she was blessed by Knowledge, the wisest of the three, so her power reads a person's time but the only thing she can interpret it as is a smell. They say all saints are bound to the three and protected by them so they are a blessed existence that no one would dare to harm. Because of this, Lilynette's maids are not fully trained ones, and she has no bodyguard as I do. Instead, she is often left with only her companion maid Nana, Anna's little sister.

Saints appear randomly in our family and extended family. That is why mother married father, to add that power to the royal bloodline. Even if she was not a saint, grandmother was and so was great grandmother; both connected to the gate like Lilynette and our cousin. Mother also told me once that she considered herself a saint because she had so much mana it rivaled heroes. She also told me of a dream she had before I was born of the 'Tree', the goddess of life, one of the three. It is not an actual tree, but that is the only thing that resembles it we know of. It is an impossibly huge tree-like thing that exists in the darkness of space and from its branches, all life is born.

In mother's dream she caught a falling fruit. It looked like an entire world was inside it and it compelled her to eat it. After eating it she saw each of the three before her: the gate, leading to the tree, leading to the spiral. After that dream I was born. Information of the three is not well known even in the church of the seven. I seem to remember. Mother told me not to talk about them to anyone else besides my children or they could curse us, also never pray to them. I wonder why that memory popped into my head suddenly? It is likely because of my brothers, oh right, she said not to tell them either, only speak of them to my daughters and sister.

"Princess, what is your opinion on the situation in the east?" Seigi-sama could tell I'm feeling left out of the discussion and asks me that question with a smile.

Don't do this, don't show Seigi such an unbecoming side of yourself; getting lost in your own thoughts and feelings. Remember, they were discussing the crops failing. This is why you spent the last week studying every historical document in the annex. Remember, what did it say about a famine fifty years ago?

"Most likely, the withering crops are a sign that the Demon Lord of the Waxing Crescent has been reborn." Everyone stops to look at me. Oh God, did I just say something stupid in front of Seigi-sama? No, his eyes aren't filled with pity but curiosity. He must have reached the same conclusion. He is perfect, figuring out the secrets of the Demon Lords just like me, even without access to the forbidden history books father has locked away.

"What is the link between the crops and the Demon Lord?" Brother is agitated, did he conclude the Demon Lord had revived but hadn't linked it to the crops? Was this a military secret? Even if it is, it's fine. Only those allowed to know such things are here.

"Sixty-four years ago there was a famine in the eastern region of the kingdom. It started as a single poor harvest and escalated from there. By the fifth year, no crops grew at all in the eastern-most regions. Our hero's knowledge was helpless in solving this crisis. Six years after the famine began, the Demon Lord of the Waxing Crescent's armies attacked. With the uniting of several heroes, the demons were vanquished after years of fighting and the famine ended.

The Demon Lord of the Waxing Crescent specializes in earth magic, the battle was detailed by Sir Siegfried in the book of heroes. Earth magic is used to make nutrient-rich soil, so it's not a stretch to think the Demon Lord associated with earth could drain the nutrients from the soil, creating a famine." It may be a leap of logic, but it is a sound theory.

"I can't believe we never made that connection. There has been an increase in demon activity and the organization with which they are acting has led us to the conclusion that the Demon Lord of the Waxing Crescent had revived. So if they follow the same strategy, it's only 3 years until they launch an invasion on our eastern border! Could this be what you were fearing, father?" We still have three years. Why is brother getting so worked up?

"May I ask? What is this book of heroes? It is the first I've heard of such a thing being mentioned. If it contains battle tactics or information on Demons it would be useful for me to read it, wouldn't it?"

"The book of heroes is managed by the church of the seven. It is a collection of writings from the many heroes since the practice of summoning them was started a thousand years ago. It is written in each of the hero's native tongue and normally only heroes are allowed access." Father stole my chance to impress Seigi. Why is he giving me that look? Is it the church? There's no point trying to hide anything from Seigi-sama. The simple fact that you are hiding it will give it away.

"The 'Church of the Seven' manages international relations between heroes and the nations they live in and fight for. They claim the heroes are gifts from the gods and that binding them to nations as we do is sacrilegious. Though they think this they still support all nations that summon heroes and a few that don't." Father is upset with the way I laid everything out but Seigi-sama would see the truth through any deception.

"The church lost a lot of power when the League of Nations formed as they were no longer the only international body that dealt with politics. In recent years they've tried to expand their power by bringing heroes under their influence instead of the country that summoned them. This has caused a lot of friction between the church and the nations responsible for hero summoning." This time Sedrik stole my chance. Why did he come back? He should have stayed on the border.

"It has been mentioned several times that other countries summon heroes. Do not all of them? Do you take turns?" The cost of summoning from beyond the gate is high. Telling heroes what that cost is too early is forbidden unless they demand the answer.

"The finer details of summoning are something only an expert would know, you can ask Roland during a future lesson. Suffice to say it isn't cheap or easy to summon a hero." Father cut me off again. I desperately studied hero summoning to answer any question Seigi-sama might have and now I'll look strange if I bring it up. Perhaps I can talk about it later with Roland.

"I will ask at some point. I would like to hear more about this church." Why? They are so boring and useless; not to mention that is where that woman works.

"We have a church liaison in the castle. You've met her many times in passing. She is working as a maid in the castle as her primary job, but she is the highest member of the church in the castle. Normally the hero is kept in relative isolation as they come to grips with their current situation. Being such an exception, you've instead opted for constant training and learning. There hasn't been a spare moment for proselytizing. If you insist, we can meet her tonight, but arch-priests are known for rising and setting with the sun.

We've set your official debut for two weeks from now. We scheduled the event with the church the same day we decided when the sum-moning would occur. It's impossible to get the highest-ranking members of the church other-wise." Ahh, Seigi-sama is focusing on me, it seems like he has questions for me since father is answer-ing in roundabout ways. I lay my soul bare before those eyes, eyes completely unlike anyone else's. They have an inhuman depth to them, like I could get lost in them forever, an endless void.

"There is no rush to meet the church, the only official duty they still have is naming the her-oes." Father is trying to change the subject again.

"Naming?" Oh, I wonder what would be a pleasant name for Seigi-sama?

"They give you an alternative name, but it is not a replacement for your own name. The church gives you an extra name. The red knight's name is 'ash' because that's what he reduces his op-ponents to. Sir Suzuki is 'the immortal' like his predecessor. He requested that name and it was eventually granted." Alphonse has stepped in this

137

time. Why did either of them come back? They aren't needed here, they're just in the way.

Seigi-sama is deep in thought. The concept of a name might be very important to him. I wonder if it would be impudent of me to suggest a name. Ufufufu, we could stay up all night discussing names; then we could set aside names for our children. Lilynette gasps loudly, drawing everyone's attention. Her eyes are showing their whites, she is trembling as she grips the table with all her might. She is heating up, her mana is running rampant. This could be dangerous. Nothing like this has ever happened before; what is wrong with her?

"With princess's tears and royal bloodshed,

this will herald," In a voice that is not her own, Lilynette speaks these lines. Even Seigi-sama trembles for a moment.

"The kingdom will tremble 4 times," Everyone is frozen mid-movement. Those that had rushed to her side stopped just before reaching her.

"Ten years of winter will end along with humanity.

Unless the hero's true power is unleashed." She let's go of the table and faints; before she falls from her chair Mia catches her and is now cradling her.

That was a divine Oracle. It is the first time I've seen one. Those are direct messages from the gate; only the most powerful of saints can give those kinds of messages. I am dragged from the room with Seigi-sama and my brothers in tow. Only mother, father and Mia are left with Lilynette. She should be fine, but what does that oracle mean? And why did Seigi-sama shiver like that at the word tears?

Mia The Head Maid

A divine oracle is always an ominous occasion. They are never wrong but not always understood in time to do anything about it. Great tragedies have been mitigated in the past but never completely averted. The one emanating from princess Lilynette tonight is no different.

"My king, the princess, and queen have retired to the princess's room, Seigi-sama and princess Releina have both gone to their rooms as well and Roland is here. I have placed another maid with the hero tonight so I can make my report in person tonight." Shanna was almost too eager to take my place tonight, but I am sure nothing of note will happen. Seigi-sama himself said that he was planning on resting after the bout earlier today, I can only imagine how much stamina it took to move that fast without the aid of magic.

"Good, Roland, have you heard the oracle?" The king's age is showing, he is visibly distraught. His heart is likely nearing its end. He had wanted to hold on long enough to allow his sons to have genuine experience in battle or to allow Lilynette to mature. Though, the queen still wants Releina to succeed him.

"Yes, my lord, we can begin with whatever you want." The king slumps into his chair and motions to Roland.

"Then Roland, I will have your report first; you may begin." The king's worried look seems to have softened a little.

"Unfortunately, Sir Seigi has made no progress with magic of any element, though he seems to understand the basic theory and structure. The problem may be his mana, it is very unusual, it feels similar in quality to the queen's and princesses' but not in quantity. He seems to lack an affinity to any element from what I can tell, it is possible he is a 'Saint.' However, his mana does not rage like princess Releina's or the queen's nor does it have a divine aura like Lilynette's; so I cannot be certain if he is a saint or not.

Sir Suzuki has stated that it reminds him of his master Sir Siegfried. His theory is that his mana is trapped within his body just like Sir Siegfried's. However, the reason and effect are most likely different since he doesn't have an affinity to holy mana. If I had to give a word to describe Sir Seigi's mana it would be dense. It is possible that it could be as much mana as princess Releina's or even more; just confined into a smaller container. These are the only possibilities that anyone has come up with as of now. I have asked the church for their records on all old saints to compare them to Sir Seigi and I will go over the chained library's catalog again for anything similar to him or the oracle.

The phenomenon like any of those theories would have untold effects on one's body with both positive and negative results happening. Going off of Sir Suzuki's theory he may be incapable of using magic similar to Sir Siegfried but would have unfathomable physical abilities or other effects that trigger automatically like Sir Siegfried's healing. This could still make him a glorious hero, but without seeing his full potential there is no way to substantiate this theory. The only thing we know for a fact is that he has already shown strength and speed surpassing our greatest soldiers while they are using strengthening magic. My estimates put him at twice the strength of the Crimson Slayer and almost twice as fast as Archduke Aranwell."

"So not terrible news, then the problem would be his weapons then?" The king's disposition has greatly improved after hearing confirmation about Seigi-sama's abilities.

"Yes your majesty, judging by his spar with Archduke Aranwell he will need an exceptional weapon to fight with his full potential. There is nothing in the royal treasury that could be used. We would have to ask the dwarven nation for a weapon of black steel and even that may not last, if, as we think, he has not shown his full strength." The dwarves. The kingdom used to have many black steel weapons, but those have all been lost to time along with the heroes that wielded them. Lost while in battle with demon lords over the centuries.

"Then we must send an envoy at once, that is all we can do at the moment. Now, Mia, your report on his mental state." All right, my turn.

"Sire, I have spent all but two nights with Sir Seigi and every waking hour with him since he was put into my care."

"Two nights you did not attend him, what happened?" A look of surprise and shock appears on both of their faces.

"On both occasions, he requested to be alone for the night to think and I stayed just outside the door, still within the range of my magic sense. I must also mention that he did not require *any* kind of emotional support, and from what I heard and detected during his nights alone he made personal attempts at using magic. The first night specifically he almost overloaded calling upon all of his mana at once. After that failure,

143

it looked as if he had something, but both times his mana was forcefully pulled back into him.

He may be feeling some kind of regret at not being able to harness it yet. I also believe that he has been pushing himself in his weapons training to compensate for the lack of progress in learning magic. Seigi-sama always has a calm demeanor and has a dominant sense of duty. I had believed that he might have been doing it to stay in our good graces. However, there have been a few instances of him showing a deeper interest in things." Now both of them are looking at me with odd expressions.

"Oh, and what might these things be?" The king looks very intrigued by this information.

"Occasionally, he looked at the princess with caring eyes; not unlike those of a suitor and also at one time he even turned those same eyes towards me." I have to make sure the king understands what I want.

"But did you not just say that he has not needed you during the night?" Roland asks quietly, shocked at this assumed contradiction.

"I said that yes, I assume that Seigi-sama is still in a bit of shock from the summoning and is focusing on his training instead of indulging in desires of the flesh. A perfect gentleman if I must say, the same cannot be said for every hero that has come. I also have a note from Sir Suzuki that during the divine oracle Sir Seigi reacted with noticeable anger and a flash of hostility at the first line mentioning the princess's tears. It is my conclusion that Seigi-sama has in some slight amount become emotionally attached to the princess and to a lesser degree myself, most likely as a kind of emotional support. It is possible we remind him of others from his home and his mind is using that similarity to anchor his thoughts."

"Oh, that is perfect, ever since Lilynette confirmed his character I had hoped to set the two of them up." The king is very pleased with this turn of events, but I must make my discovery clearer to him.

"Unfortunately, Sire it may not be so perfect, you may think this contradicts my prior statement, but Seigi-sama has never once looked at the princess with any kind of lust or desire. As for myself, for the first few days when we were alone, Sir Seigi would observe me intensely. I am sure he has discovered my purpose and some of my training and chose to remain cordial for now. With this in mind, I would like to request that if the princess cannot capture him, I be permitted the next attempt." This is my goal, the princess will fail and I can have him all to myself. Not that

I would mind sharing with her. Princess Releina is too inexperienced and I am sure Seigi-sama has had plenty from what I can tell.

"My, my this hero is popular, to have even enticed Miss Mia. I guess those rumors from the other maids were true." Roland, making conjecture again. Those girls are getting ahead of themselves again; all of them will need discipline.

"Mia, I plan on giving Releina plenty of time to try but I promise you the opportunity if she fails. I would love to see my daughter happy, but it is never good to force these things too hard with heroes. Now then, if that is the end of your report, let's move on." At least the king is entertaining the idea of her failing, but how long is he going to make me wait?

"Sire, then I shall repeat the divine oracle,

'With princess's tears and royal bloodshed, this will herald,
The kingdom will tremble 4 times,
Ten years of winter will end along with humanity,
Unless the hero's true power is unleashed.'

We have already sent a copy to the church and I have my two best intelligence workers comparing it to past oracles we have records of.

Though I expect little of that investigation, oracles are abstract so the best we can hope for is to glean some clearer meaning from a few words."

"The first line is the most troubling as it implies we cannot stop it, regardless Mia, I want you to double Lilynette's guard. I am sure Suzuki is already on high alert. I will let nothing happen to my daughters if it is within my power to prevent it. Roland, how are the repairs to the castle defenses?"

"Unfortunately slow, the hero summoning shattered the large holy circle in the basement. To not expose our weakness, my team has been repairing the outermost circles first. It will take at least a month before everything is back to normal." The amount of mana used in summoning Seigi-sama caused an immense surge of mana in all the castle's magic circles. This overwhelming amount of mana made some of them burn out damaging the circles, many beyond repair, all of them need to be replaced.

"Mia, call back any reserves we have for the month and don't let this news spread outside of the castle. Informing the church was the right call. They will send help, but no one outside of the castle staff may know of the oracle until the defenses are back up. Do either of you have any thoughts on the rest of the oracle?"

"I believe that the kingdom will be hit with 4 great tragedies, the first one is likely connected to the first line. As for the ten-year winter and the end of humanity. I think it is not one of the tragedies, so it is likely not an actual winter since that in itself could end humanity. I believe it is a war with the demons at worst and a great famine or drought at best." These are not the only possibilities, but these are things we can prepare for by calling upon our allies to the west. The chances that we cannot determine the oracles' meaning are high so we can only do what is possible and not worry about what is impossible.

"My thoughts are similar, I fear that we cannot prepare because of the 4 tragedies. So we must put it all into the last line, Sir Seigi is the key, I will search the archives for any information on a suitable weapon for him and put in a few orders for black steel weapons using my funds for now. I would not want to tax the treasury for something that may not work out. Also, since I have no heir I do not mind spending on Sir Seigi." Roland's decision shows resolve; he is almost fatherly right now. It seems he too is fond of Seigi-sama.

"Yes, we will do what we can then, the border forts are already on high alert. I will increase guard shifts for the castle till the defenses are back, but I fear it will not be enough. If Seigi needs anything, don't hesitate. He may be our only hope here, I permit you to inform him of what we have discussed at your discretion, Mia. You have your orders dismissed."

"Yes, Sir" The two of us answer at the same time.

I will return to Seigi-sama once I have sent out the new orders. Then I will explain the situation well into the night if I must. Omitting anything regarding the princess or myself. No need to be fair and open when it comes to the princess. As they say, all is fair in love and war.

Seigi

That night I received an in-depth briefing about the oracle and the king's plan for the future regarding equipping me with a suitable weapon from the dwarven nation far to the southwest. Demi-human races seem to be in the kingdom, but dwarves and elves appear to stay in the mountains and forests, respectively. Humans that have animal features seem to live everywhere that humans do, just in varying numbers.

While they live in the kingdom, they are a minority here. They are a minority everywhere aside from two nations far to the west, where they appear to have gathered but by unnatural means. I was also told that there are many races normally working in the castle, but they are slowly introduced to heroes as they have an array of reactions to the unique races.

Ever since then I have redoubled my training; at least with my weapon training. I have become proficient in every weapon in the royal armory. Though, some mid-range weapons don't seem to work very well with my extra strength. The chain scythe, flail, and lance would only allow me to use half the strength that I used with a sword or other close-range weapons. I have also become well versed in various throwing weapons, even some that are not meant for throwing.

Since most weapons will break after a few hits I practiced throwing them as their last use. Learning fresh things always comes easy for me, but I am surprised at the ease of learning the art of killing. Humans have killed throughout their entire history, but I had thought it was a trait people of my era had to work hard to get in our modern-day and age. This again makes me wonder if they were right about me.

Two weeks passed in the blink of an eye, and now we have come to my official presentation to the nation. The church has sent a high-priest, various nobles from the nation's largest provinces, and a few other official-looking people from the church are here for the ceremony. These types of events have never been enjoyable for me, however, they are more for the people watching than those taking part. I understand that appearances matter in all societies.

Now that I am one of the important people of this world these kinds of things will become the norm so I must endure. Releina looks happy watching from the side, I had assumed she would be with me here since she summoned me. I have still not completely grasped this nation's culture, partly because of their imposed isolation. Their system of easing one into society has some merit for normal people that are slow to adapt. Unfortunately, this just annoys me to no end. I like to resolve what I can fast, having to wait weighs on my mind.

The social etiquette in this room is following a class system, anyone with a lower station is greeting all those above them before getting into position for the ceremony to begin. None of the nobles are greeting any of the three heroes here or any members of the royalty. I can only guess that we are in a higher tier that cannot be disturbed before we begin. Also, the lowest rank here, servants have on featureless white masks this seems to be two-fold to prevent unpleasant nobles from belittling the servants and to help them maintain composure around those same troublesome nobles.

Neither Mia nor Anna are visible. I doubt they would serve this event since apparently castle maids hold a prominent position compared to normal servants. All of them are noble's daughters or were high-ranking members of the military before becoming maids. I had guessed that they had more duties than just normal housework, Mia and Anna especially given how they carry themselves. They likely are watching over princess Lilynette since she is not here. I recall Mia saying something alluding to that when she left me here.

Some miscellaneous pageantry has begun, nothing I am concerned with but I have to move into position to be received. Suddenly, the oddest feeling befalls me. A few presences in the room feel different, there is no way for me to describe this feeling. But five people who were here feel like they became other people. Is this some kind of magic? The room seems to have slowed down as well, I know this feeling. Those unfamiliar presences are hostile. Is this what killing intent feels like? I will have to make a note of this. My gaze first turns to Suzuki to see if he has noticed. He is moving slowly just like everyone else, but his face shows that he noticed it.

Then I look for the red knight since he is also a hero, he is also slowed down, but not as much as Suzuki, he is moving toward the door with a very cocky grin. How detestable, he seems to know what is happening or at the very least is happy it is happening. Those persons that are releasing this killing intent are moving to the royal family, ah a coup. Well, is that not auspicious? If I can stop them that should help me fit into my position as a hero better. Those people are not moving as slow as everyone else; what is with this?

Having decided what my response will be I reach for my sword, but damn, I am moving relatively slow as well. It seems only my mind is accelerated, my body is moving just a bit faster than the other heroes. Currently, my movements appear just about as fast as those assassins, how unfortunate. At this speed I cannot intercept any of them. This could be bad. I will have to rethink my plans.

If they kill the royal family, what would that mean for me? Even if I stop the coup, this country will fall into chaos, a hero cannot allow that. So I have to save at least one of them. I will have to throw my sword, I will no longer have a weapon, but one of them must live. The princess is the only option, if I kill her assassin then Suzuki can get her to safety. He is not quick, but he is moving in this state. Yes, that has to work, I throw my sword using as much strength and speed as I can at the assassin aiming for Releina.

In that instant all the assassins quake with fear but only briefly; they continue on their course, very professional if I must say so. Just like the assassins that went after father-in-law, I should also note that I am still wearing my black suit and have been throughout my training. While it looks like a normal business suit, it is a specialty made with carbon nanofibers and many other materials and special techniques. That makes it bulletproof, knife proof, and it is insulated against heat, cold and it can even protect against tasers, all while still being an easy fit.

Meaning even without a weapon or armor I am far from defenseless, in this world of sword and sorcery it would surprise me if this is not nigh-indestructible aside from maybe magic. Back home these suits had a lifetime guarantee since their jobs were to protect the lives of many of the world's most influential people and fittingly they cost over a billion yen.

The suit I have is a copy of suits that were said to be worn by the US Secret Service. They say it is almost as good as modern combat body armor but not as confining, allowing for a full range of motion so it is easy to fight in. Father-in-law had many enemies, so all of his top executives have these suits and simple self-defense training. Nothing like the training I have had since getting here, no, just how to get out of holds and how to escape from assassins. Never once, while I was making my plans with Haruno, did I think working in pharmaceuticals could have been as dangerous as it turned out to be.

While this was happening the red knight was none the wiser having not even noticed. He is busy closing the entrance. The assassin that was aiming for Releina with resolve in his eyes continued his path with the mission of killing Releina, however before his dagger could reach her, the sword I threw with all my might pierced straight through him. The force of the impact also forced him away from her, splattering his body against the wall behind her. The sword tore a chunk out of the wall and shattered. As I take my first human life I feel nothing, I wonder if it is because they are an enemy and had to die to save her or is this also something I lack?

A moment later Suzuki has her in his arms and is running for the window; by then the daggers of the other assassins stab into the hearts of the royal family. The remaining assassins show their professionalism, right after stabbing their targets they twist the dagger for an instant kill. All of them move away instantly, but then just as suddenly as it began they appear to freeze. Have they slowed down?

The red knight and Suzuki are the only ones moving now, though very slowly still. The look on Releina's face shows she is processing what is going on and what just happened to her family. Ah, everyone else in the room now has a look of shock on their faces, I guess everything is going back to normal? The assassin's speed earlier must have been a temporary ability. There is no way they would have stopped using something so useful if they did not have to.

My mind seems to be returning to normal

speed, well as normal as I have been since coming here, anyway. The first sound I hear after returning to normal speed is that of Releina screaming in terror. Yeah, from that position she just saw almost all of her family killed in front of her. That is a terrifying sight, but there was nothing I could do, I only had one sword. Oh! What? Is she, is she crying? Yes, this too makes sense, doesn't it? It looks like they made her cry...

Now, what to do? The main entrance sealed itself, it fused with the wall; the windows slowly close themselves. This is the security system the princess was so proud of. Saying that, she defended the castle with these automatic defenses. *Crash* A window shatters as Suzuki jumps through it just before it closes carrying the princess, well, like a princess.

The remaining assassins have all escaped through a window on the opposite side of the room just as it is sealed with magic. Despite obviously being professional, they didn't even try to finish the job. They must not be able to deal with Suzuki in a normal fight, meaning I can entrust her safety to him.

Ok, let's calmly go over the situation, while everyone else in the room is panicking. A coup is happening, the red knight and a few nobles have declared such. They said they are also attacking key places around the nation besides the capital, but that is irrelevant to me right now. Roland is enraged and launches some kind of magic at the red knight, but it just breaks on him like water crashing onto rocks. He has flames wrapped around him; he is not the red knight for nothing. He then throws what looks like a javelin made of fire at Roland and Roland bursts into flames leaving only ashes behind; his extra name makes sense too.

The nobles and knights not part of the coup look terrified. Most look to me for guidance but I have yet to decide what to do so I ignore them. Someone on the red knight's side proclaims to have won and is demanding that everyone surrender or die, how cliche. These idiots made the princess cry for such a stupid reason as not being treated fairly by the crown. With such a weak premise these people here are not the mastermind behind the coup, these people cannot articulate themselves well enough to lead a coup.

That appears to be the situation. We are all sealed in here till the princess opens it up, she dies, or uses up all her mana. Even being drained far faster than normal Roland said before that Releina had more than enough mana to seal the castle for weeks or months. That means I need to get out of here fast and help anyone still alive outside. Unfortunately, I don't know if I can beat the red knight's magic. Fire is very dangerous. Should I try and use my magic? If it really is death magic, then this should be easy and if it is not, then I can find out if I can reveal it to everyone without worry.

No one seems to mind me right now. Only the red knight is looking at me, all pissed off. The nobles are just glancing at me a little, in between their talks with the other nobles. Some knights look like they want to do something but are waiting for me. I don't have a weapon anymore but I could get one from someone close by so the problem now is that I do not think I can save anyone if I get into a fight with the red knight. Fire is too wild and dangerous, I guess they are all forfeit. No need to think about that.

"The princess escaped with the old Hero so even with the king and other royals dead the kingdom will not collapse, now I just have to survive...... I guess that makes everyone in this room expendable." My face and body completely relax as I say this, once again dropping my mask.

Having already decided everyone here must die, I need not worry about keeping it up now. Everyone seems to have noticed this significant change in demeanor and they already look afraid of me. This is just as I expected. People here are the same as back home. Once I drop my mask, they become terrified. Figuring this was happening anyway I decided I should gather all the information I can which includes people's reaction to my 'default' self and my magic and finding out its true effects.

"This narrative can work. All tragedies can be blamed on these fools and only successes will be attributed to me, the hero. Yes, that kind of story should work in any world, humans love a pleasant story." While I say this, I pause to give everyone time to process what is happening and allow me to see all of their different reactions.

"Hmm, how can I make this the most believable? Should I mutilate the corpses? Hey, minister of whatever. Of those who refuse to submit, would they mutilate your corpses before displaying them to the public?" After a moment of shock, one of the King's ministers answers.

"No, they would want the corpses in as pristine condition as possible. To better recognize them and show how merciful they were." The man has a dumbfounded face as he answers me completely disregarding what that question implies.

"Oh, so that's how it works. It's good I asked, my narrative would have been to showcase their cruelty, but if that diverges too much from the expected reality then it won't be easily accepted." The red knight is looking pale and confused, it seems he cannot keep up with the situation.

Flames gather around him, that must be another form of his magic, the searing temperature forces everyone away, he is furious and losing control.

"That's enough out of you. Look around you. You have no allies and no escape option. Your only choices are to surrender peacefully or die." Look at that. The floor is melting around him. Still, not knowing what my magic does means I should test it before fighting him.

"You would normally be right, but that's assuming you and your lot are capable of subduing me. Though I'll have to kill everyone here as my method of defeating you has to be kept secret. With me as the only survivor, I open up a number of alternative paths, all of which still has me being the hero and you just a traitor to the crown."

The red knight then sends a wave of fire at my legs, ok time to work, I call forth my mana it spirals out from my heart and flows out of me to meet his. If it doesn't stop it, I can leap away with time to spare, considering how slow it's moving. The flames crash against my mana and disperse harmlessly. Now I have a cloak of shadowy black mist around me, much like his cloak of flames.

I feel even lighter than before and I can see the smallest little white flame inside everyone here; it seems I have magic sight when mana is flowing through me. And it seems those stories were right. This death magic consumes magic and a person's life force. A high-pitched shriek interrupts my thoughts. The High Priest representing the church is trying to crawl further into the corner he was hiding in as he stutters out some words.

"D, D-D-DEMON!!!" Like I have never heard that before. The old man is frantically clawing at the walls as though he's trying to dig his way out of the room. His panic is rapidly spreading to the others.

"Don't bother. The room magically sealed itself the moment the king died. Only other royalty can deactivate the seal to enter or leave. That's why these guys have been so sure of themselves." That old man from before is still shrieking in terror he is getting annoying.

"It's the Demon Lord of the New Moon." The noble leading this coup whispers.

"When did you replace the summoned hero?" He continues.

"An interesting misunderstanding has occurred. Which confirms it was the right decision to hide my magic and that I can't leave any witnesses. Well, time to get down to business." Focusing my mana into my hand, I give will to the shadows surrounding me and they engulf the people behind me, finally some quiet, no more of that annoying shrieking. Good, it kills instantly and leaves no noticeable marks if I didn't know better I would think they just fell asleep. Now that I am sure of the effects I can use it in battle without worry.

The red knight has lost any composure he might have still had and expands his flame cloak to what I assume is his maximum power. Again I focus my mana into my hand and send the mist at the rest of them. It extinguishes his flames, one noble let out an anguished gasp and everyone but the red knight falls to the ground.

"Interesting, by enveloping yourself in magic you managed to save your life. It would be valuable to continue to experiment. However, I apparently can't negate the heat from that pool of lava you've created. So I'll end this now." I release two pulses, this time in quick succession that should finish him. In less than the beat of a heart the pool of lava expands, but it is too late, his magic is gone and then his life. The red knight lets out a small sigh as he falls. This cannot be everyone involved with this coup, I still have a lot of work to do.

With everyone in the room dead I go about setting up the proper narrative, desecrating the corpse as would be fit for a proper battle, giving out wounds where needed with various weapons from everyone here. Even after killing all these people and mangling their bodies, I still feel nothing for them. There was a possibility I would have enjoyed killing them, but luckily that emotion never rose. I simply felt like they were nothing.

That is when I hear a small gasp coming from the thrones. I rush over quickly and see the queen's chest rising slowly and blood oozing out of her chest wound very slowly. From what I can see it is a fatal wound. How is she not dead? She turns her head to look at me. I have my default face still on and I bring my mana out, but she smiles at me causing my body and mind to freeze. Not a moment later with a smile on her face, she breathes her last, as I am still frozen in shock. Her smile, that look on her face, she looked exactly like that little one did way back then. How? Why? It doesn't matter; she is gone, just like that little one.

I take all the weapons in the room. There are only five short swords and the red knight's long broadsword. The most interesting thing I found are four small belts of throwing knives. They are all that is left of the assassin's corpse besides some scattered limbs. These could be very useful, if I had had these I might have been able to save all of them. With the room all set, I just have to get out and put an end to this coup. The magic that seals this room repairs any damage done, but I should be able to break out, regardless. Let's use this to check how strong I am. Moving over to the wall facing outside, I prepare myself. There should be no one that could get hit by debris, so full strength.

Bam With one swift punch the wall is gone, it doesn't even look like there was sizable debris, just dust. Not very good data, but a single data point would not be enough, anyway. I hear fighting coming from all around me so lets trust Suzuki with the princess and put out these small fires. The closest one is to the left, I jump into one of the lower windows and start running toward the sound of fighting. Changing my face to number 11 should work well for this. Yes, that should help the situation flow nicely. Showing slight anger should be enough to intimidate, to reveal friends and foes easily.

Once I come up upon the group of knights fighting half look happy and the rest look terrified, they are making this easy. With a single swing, I bisect the terrified knights and continue racing down the hall. Every group reacts the same way, they don't know how to hide their emotions in this world. Even holding back I can finish them easily using the red knight's sword while not breaking it. Once again I feel nothing taking their lives; each swing of my sword ending a person forever. It doesn't take long to snuff out every minor fire inside the castle, in due time all fighting in the castle has stopped and the guards remove the bodies. Finished with the cleanup, I am heading to the secret safe room the princess told me was for emergencies to make sure she is safe.

How was I supposed to let them know everything is fine? There should be a way they can hear me, I knock I believe the door was supposed to be while slightly raising my voice.

"Princess Releina, the castle is secure please open the door!" The wall glows and opens. Suzuki is pushing the door open and looks at me with a somber face; I still have number 11 on, that should be fine for this situation, they will interpret the anger differently. Once the door is open, the princess runs to embrace me. It seems she started crying once she saw me. Why am I feeling so off about this situation?

I notice that princess Lilynette, Mia, and Anna are in the back of the safe room too. Trying to calm princess Releina I place my hand atop her head saying to her and the others.

"I have taken care of all enemy forces within the castle. But based on the information I obtained from the red knight, they have forces attacking key facilities around the kingdom. Sir Suzuki, I would ask you to leave the princesses' safety to me for some time so you can see to the military response within the capital immediately. The castle may be secure but I doubt the situation is the same everywhere else."

"I understand Sir Seigi, and what of the red knight and the rest of the people in the throne room?"

"It was unfortunate but during my fight with the red knight everyone else perished, I was not strong enough to save them."

"Please, don't look down on yourself, Sir Seigi. I am not confident that I would have been able to defeat Mikeal in that situation myself. Mia, please come with me. We must issue orders immediately Sir Seigi and Anna can keep the princesses safe."

"Yes, at once Sir Suzuki." Mia and Suzuki race off, I can leave defending the capital to them.

"Anna let's take them both to Releina's

room for tonight." She nods and saying nothing, she carries the sobbing Lilynette off toward Releina's room.

Princess Releina is still crying and clinging to me, why does this feel familiar, this is the first time I have ever seen her crying, right? Is the contrast between now and how she normally is messing with my perception? I gently lift her in a normal princess carry and follow Anna. Lilynette has fallen asleep in Anna's arms by the time we reach Releina's room. Once in Releina's room Anna placed Lilynette on the bed and grabbed a chair from the table and moved it to the side of the bed. I set Princess Releina down on the other side and she lets go of me, as I turn to leave the room she grabs my coat timidly before I move away.

"Please, Seigi-sama, stay with us, just for to-night." Princess Releina says with a very haggard face, and Anna moves another chair between the bed and the door, with both the door and window in its view. Looks like I am stuck here. I change to number 5 and hold her hand in mine and respond.

"Princess Releina, you have my word that I will watch over you all night. Now please get some rest; tomorrow will bring many more challenges. Ones that I, unfortunately, cannot help you with." Releina's face changes to one of acceptance and gratitude. She seems almost calm now and with that lays her head down and immediately falls asleep. Is this how you are supposed to comfort someone? I don't have enough data so I will just have to wait and see.

Checking on Anna, I see that she is just sitting quietly watching the two of them with an appropriately sad face on, so I change back to number 11 and go to my chair. Once I sit down I feel a grand weight set upon me and extreme exhaustion comes out of nowhere. Perhaps I used too much magic? For the first time since coming here, I wish I could sleep but I have to watch over the princesses. While not as painful as my first night trying out magic I am far more exhausted. As I begin my guard duty a thought passes through my head, I wonder if I was able to do that for "her" would things have turned out differently?

Suzuki

It's finally the date for Seigi's, Hero's Welcome, an official introduction to the nation and the world. At this point, I had only spoken to my mentor, my summoner, and my maid for a little over a month's time. I'm sure I met the then-current king and queen as Seigi did, but I can't say I spoke with them. Seigi has already formed some kind of relationship with everyone in the castle. He even spoke to the church liaison for an entire night. Mia was present the entire time so we know nothing besides proselytizing happened. The thought that they would try to take him or make a pass at him worried Princess Releina.

Unfortunately, Seigi has stopped making any progress in his training this last week. He is more than proficient in every weapon, but without a skilled master, he can't get better. If he were to take part in actual combat, he might perfect his style, but we can't exactly send him off to war. He continues to make no progress in magic, which the church won't be happy about.

Though the most pressing matter for me is that the princess hasn't been able to make any progress. They show significant chemistry and it's obvious he has feelings towards her, but I'm fearing Mia is right and it's closer to the bonds of a sister than a lover. With how in love she is and that prophecy, I'm fearing the worst. The king is considering forcing the matter, but conventional wisdom says you shouldn't force this, especially with new heroes.

The lesser nobles are all here, the ceremony can finally begin. Seigi continues to astound me. He moves with absolute confidence, fulfilling everything expected from him in high society without the arrogance of the nobles who view it as a birthright. He even shows the occasional mistake or flaw, which is enough for the proudest nobles to save face. Could he be doing this on purpose? Mia believes everything he shows us is a fabrication based on what's expected of him and his true self is seen in flashes and is far more vulnerable. He has not talked about his life back home, but I am sure he is from an affluent family with an extensive history.

All this pageantry is still a pain, even after all these years. Some of us never get used to it. A wave of discomfort washes over me. Powerful magic was just evoked. I don't know what is going on but my body is already moving towards the princess. Without looking, I count five hostile presences inside this room. How the hell did they get here? One is right by the princess, I won't make it in time, they are moving impossibly fast. My body feels so old right now.

I'm moving beyond my top speed but I was careless, I allowed too much space between us. Suddenly there is a flash of steel before my eyes and the assassin next to the princess is impaled. I feel the rush of wind following long after the blade. The assassin was completely obliterated, their remains now cover the wall. Sir Seigi is in a throwing stance, it was his sword. I'm sorry Sir Seigi, it is thanks to you I can fulfill my purpose but I must abandon you to whatever is occurring here.

Moving beyond what I am normally capable of, I grab the princess as the other assassins drive their blades into the rest of her family. Their magic has worn off, there is no chance of pursuit. Though it would be foolish to believe this is the end. The door is already sealed and the windows are slowly closing. I throw myself with the princess out the closest window.

The courtyard appears empty. No, it was empty. Already soldiers are coming out of the castle. It's obvious, but they were prepared for at least me to escape. Taking the twenty-meter drop as best I can, I land with the princess in tears. The last I noticed from the throne room was a burst of icy anger likely coming from Sir Seigi, in that instant I felt dread like never before, it was undoubtedly his wrath leaking.

My ankles are both destroyed and my right shin snaps while my left knee explodes based on the pain I feel from it. But the princess is unharmed, I was able to completely absorb the impact. Ignoring the pain I stand back up, this level of pain is within my capabilities to suppress. I need to act fast. Letting the princess drop to the ground, I draw my sword and intercept the soldiers. They are woefully outmatched. I may no longer be a match for Sir Seigi, but anyone not clad in magic doesn't stand a chance. Muscles tear as I push my unprepared body to its limits, taking down a dozen soldiers in the courtyard. It was a very painful warm-up, but it seems I'm in the clear for now. I grab the princess and head to the safe room.

I don't know who is hostile, so activating any of the auto defenses could be disastrous. More soldiers are rushing down the corridor. I can't risk them being hostile. We take a different path, I never memorized the secret paths, they change and I am not good at remembering those kinds of patterns and the princess is in shock. A hand reaches out from the wall behind me. If I wasn't on such high alert, it would have caught me by surprise. I grab the arm and pin its owner against the now solid wall I pulled her from.

"Mia!"

"I apologize for startling you Sir Suzuki but may I ask you to release me; we don't have time to stand in the open." I release her and only afterward spend a moment wondering if she is part of this coup. I dismiss the thought as quickly as it comes. There are exactly 4 people I can be certain aren't involved outside of the Royal family. Mia drags me and the princess into the wall. It's one of the paths to the safe room.

"Sir Suzuki, hostile soldiers are swarming through the castle. They have captured the summoning room and at least one defense room. What happened to the King?" Releina twitches when she hears Mia ask about her father.

I can tell she figured out the answer to her question even as she asked it. There would be no reason for me to be with Releina outside right now.

"It's a coup. Sir Joffrey appears to be the leader, he has Mikeal! There were assassins mixed in with the servants for tonight's event. I couldn't stop any of them. If not for Sir Seigi I would have failed my duty."

"You abandoned Sir Seigi with Mikeal?" Her

voice rises and her face becomes flushed, but we do not have time for anger.

"I had no choice, even if we stood our ground protecting the princess in such a confined place would have been impossible against Mikeal. I don't know the intricacies of their plan, but as long as the princess is safe, their coup has failed. We need to get her to the safe room. From there we can commence a purging if we believe the castle has fallen." There is anger in my voice, I shouldn't be directing it at Mia.

Mia guides us through various seldom-used corridors and secret passages. We encounter no one. Until four guards are standing around what appears to be an ordinary wall.

"Are they with the coup or are they with us?" I ask Mia for her opinion. As head maid, she is far more familiar with the new personnel than I.

"It doesn't matter, if they are standing here they are ignoring orders or following someone else's. Dispose of them." I can follow her logic, though I wish we could get some allies at this juncture. Logically no one should be in this part of the castle, I keep telling myself.

From our hiding spot, I rush out ambushing the men. I bury my blade deep in the first's skull before they even notice me. The second falls just as easily, but I hear glass shattering. A purple mist is rising from the ground. Poison? It won't affect me, but it could make bringing the princess in difficult. As I ready my sword, the surrounding air ignites. It has been a very long time since I was set ablaze and I had hoped that it would never happen again. Scalding air fills my lungs, but at least it's air. Green and purple lines light up the corridor and a cooling breeze clears the air. The princess appears to have calmed down and regained control of the castle.

"Mia, you could have warned me. Even if I won't die, I still feel pain like a normal person. Burning alive is the worst kind of pain." It hurts even more as I feel my lungs regenerate.

"It was a rapidly dispersing airborne poison. I had no choice but to react quickly. It seems seeing you in such a state has broken the princess's shock." Releina looks better than before.

"Mia, how is my sister? I believe Anna was in charge of her during the events today." The princess is putting up a strong front. Based on the way Mia's face contorted for an instant, the answer might break that front.

"Unfortunately, I learned things were amiss when the communication system the maids used stopped functioning. After confirming the nursery was sealed off, I have contacted no one outside this group." Releina wavered, I need to say something, anything that would allow her to trick herself into being strong.

"It's possible Anna made it here with the little princess already, which is why those guards were standing outside." I can't even convince myself, but my feeble words are propping up the princess for now.

She forces the door open. Within is a sizable space fitted with some very luxurious furniture and provisions fit for Royalty. On a two-seater couch is Anna with Lilynette crying into her lap. Anna looks relieved that the door is open but seeing our state her expression sours. The relief on Releina's face is heartbreaking. This will probably be the last pleasant news she has in years. We file in, Mia hangs back to cremate the corpses outside. Then we seal the room. Based on what I saw in the throne room, there isn't another living being that can open this room from the outside.

Anna made tea for the princesses to calm them. Lilynette has stopped crying, but the gentlest breeze could shatter this false peace. It's been almost an hour since the coup began. While I can take some solace in knowing it has failed because we made it here with Releina. Not knowing how far the damage has spread is almost as bad as knowing the minimum that was already done.

"Sir Suzuki, what are our options? The longer this drags out, the more likely it is that we are the only ones left. How do we proceed from here?" Mia has been furious since I told her we left Seigi in the throne room.

"They had to have at least enough forces to take the entire castle, however, our secretly increased forces can overturn this situation. If they came with overwhelming numbers, the reinforcements won't help but they will slow them down. If we allow for error, after three hours the battle should be decided and they will come for us. That is when we will confront the first problem. I assume they will try to convince us that our side won. Regardless of the true victor, the ones coming for us will claim to be allies. If they don't, it will be a godsend as the princess can cleanse the castle and we can begin a counter-attack.

Either way, she will need to cleanse the castle; the only difference is if we give them time to clear the castle or try to take them all down. Then it's the counter-attack. With the King dead, emergency procedures have been activated. This will ensure that the princess and I alone can hold the castle for years. However, I have no idea what to do after that. There has never been a coup like this before, we don't know how the other nobles will react to this. They may side with our enemies."

"Regardless of the victor, to secure our stability we will have to rely on our allies to the west if we cannot rely on the nobles here. They are greedy fools, but they don't want to face the threat of the Demons so they will prop us up. That will only ensure the princess's rule, to save the nation we may have to sell the little princess in a political marriage to get back on our feet. There will be many offers, she is guaranteed to be beautiful, has a confirmed skill and the blood of heroes. This will be a very harsh future for the two, but it may be better to get the little princess out of here fast; as there are three more disasters on the way."

Oh God, I forgot about the prophecy in this confusion. Wait, if Sir Seigi perished was he not the hero mentioned or is humanity doomed? The ten-year winter may be ended by the summoning of a new hero. I push the thought from my mind. I can't be bothered with the prophecy I need to focus on the crisis at hand.

Time passes agonizingly slowly. It should still be another hour at the earliest before we receive word from the victor. Despite this, we hear a resounding thud from the door.

"Princess Releina, the castle is secure

please open the door." It's Sir Seigi, that's impossible. Did he defeat Mikeal? The princess is fumbling to stand. I push the door open and she practically flies into his arms. Finally, she is allowing herself to cry.

"I have taken care of all enemy forces within the castle. But based on the information I obtained from the red knight, they have forces attacking key facilities around the kingdom. Sir Suzuki, I would ask you to leave the princesses' safety to me for some time so you can see to the military response within the capital immediately. The castle may be secure but I doubt the situation is the same everywhere else." He not only defeated Mikeal but extracted information from him. Then he went on to single-handedly suppress all of their forces in the castle. Who the hell were you Seigi? And not a drop of blood on you.

"I understand Sir Seigi, and what of the red knight and the rest of the people in the throne room?"

"It was unfortunate but during my fight with the red knight everyone else perished, I was not strong enough to save them." He looks honestly sad that he couldn't protect them. Is this that vulnerability Mia spoke of that appears occasionally?

"Please, don't look down on yourself Sir Seigi. I am not confident that I would have been able to defeat Mikeal in that situation myself. Mia, come with me. We must issue orders immediately Sir Seigi and Anna can keep the princesses safe."

"Yes, at once Sir Suzuki." There is a surprising number of people still in the castle. I don't know how Sir Seigi decided which side they were on, but I'll trust his judgment. Guards are already clearing the dead.

Between Mia and me, we get the castle running and contact the various border forts. The worst hasn't come to pass. Most of the forts respond, telling of their repelling an attack or that there have been no problems. I wring oaths of loyalty to Releina out of the northern and western border nobles by mentioning that Sir Seigi defeated Mikeal. They probably would have sworn fealty at the coronation, but I can't risk further insurrection. The east agreed with only the first prompt. The problem is the south, the other forts recognize Releina as the queen but backed off when I pushed an oath. Damn snakes playing both sides. We won't be able to expect their help in reestablishing control.

I've laid the groundwork for several contingencies. They are just waiting for an order from the new queen. It seems they attacked very few places. They likely planned on tricking the other nobles with lies. I'm worried about those assassins. That magic allowed them to enter and surpass the realm of heroes. This is troubling on many levels. In an hour the scouts should report the movements of the fleeing rebels. Joffrey was one of Archduke Aranwell's closest men, while I hope he hasn't turned; one fort that didn't respond was his. If only Roland had survived. There would be more options available to us. I hate having to push the hard decisions off onto an inexperienced girl, but that is why Royalty exists. Once I notice the time I give Mia the order.

"Mia, it is almost dawn. Please fetch the princess. Give her all the time she needs to prepare herself. But be timely, the faster we act the better our chances." Now the actual fight begins; her first test as queen is putting down a full-blown rebellion.

Seigi The Next Morning

Dawn breaks, there were no urgent reports during the night so Suzuki must have been able to deal with everything. Once Releina wakes up, she will have a tough job ahead of her. I wonder what the most efficient way to deal with this will be? Hopefully, Suzuki and Mia have plenty of information on what is happening within the kingdom so this can be handled swiftly. My fatigue from the night before is gone. I did not sleep at all, but just resting my body was enough. That is some useful information.

Anna has been up all night. Every once in a while she would glance at me but then immediately return her gaze to the princesses. She is worried about them, during the night Lilynette grabbed her hand and has not let go of it since. As a bit of light from the window fills the room, I see Releina stir, I cannot see her face from this angle so I cannot be sure if she has awoken. Anna gets up from her chair and moves to Releina's side, which causes Lilynette to stir as well. Anna helps Releina sit on the bed; her tears have dried, but she still has quite the somber face. I change to number 5 to greet them and Releina makes eye contact with me, then slightly blushes.

"Good morning Princesses, I hope you are well-rested." Lilynette has also sat up by herself and is looking around a little confused.

"Thanks to you Seigi-sama, I honestly did not think I would have been able to sleep at all if it was not for you being here." She sounds honest but there is no sorrow in her voice like yesterday, could she be over their deaths already or is she concealing it better?

"Then I will wait just outside the door for both of you to get ready." I stand up and exit the room, after I close the door I can hear Lilynette crying once more, I return to using number 11. A few moments later Mia comes running down the hall.

"Seigi-sama have you been out here all night?" She looks shocked and worried.

"Ah no, the princesses just woke up, so I left the room. I fulfilled my duty and watched them all night with Anna. If I may, it seems the capital is well under control."

"Yes, once word had spread that the castle was safe, the rebels in the capital retreated south. I will give you the full report with Princess Releina in the briefing room once she is ready."

Mia enters the room once she knocks and announces herself at my request, I would not want to have any kind of misunderstanding during this kind of situation. Their culture of not knocking is seemingly set up to have those kinds of accidents as a common occurrence. At the very least, I will not be dealing with that of my own accord. About an hour later, Mia and Princess Releina emerged from the room. Releina has a stern look on her face now; almost like she is going to war. In a way, I guess she is, isn't she? Lilynette will be cared for by Anna, for now at least. It seems her maids were trapped in the nursery during the coup.

"I will lead the way please princess, Seigi-sama, this way." Mia leads us to a room on a floor of the castle I have never been to before. There are several people gathered along the walls here talking into their hands next to some glowing magic circles, I guess there is some kind of long-distance communication network set up in this world after all. Suzuki is at a large table in the middle of the room adjusting a map.

"Princess Releina!" Suzuki announces her and the room falls silent; half the people rise and bow to her as she enters the room. So they bow here, they must only use it in wartime since I have seen no one do it before now.

"Princess if you are ready, I have the most up-to-date information ready for you."

"Sir Suzuki, If you would start at the beginning, please."

"...Yes, princess, at approximately the same time as the attack on the castle three of the major front line forts to the south and east were attacked from the inside and a couple of reserve supply bases just south of the capital. We did not receive any reports from two of the other southern forts, so we believe that their forces are part of the coup as well and have in essence already fallen. But some good news, we repelled every insurgent force. There are many casualties, but all the forts and bases have reported that our forces remain in control of all facilities and that the insurgents have retreated.

Just a few hours ago we have confirmed that all enemy units appear to be heading south to the largest of the fallen forts. Fort Armor, which is directly under the control of Archduke Jin Aranwell. It would be safe to say that he is the mastermind of this coup. As for the assassins, we have no information about their identities or their current location, they are most likely foreigners, and have likely fled the country or went to Fort Armor along with the other retreating forces."

"How long until we can muster a response to them?" Releina asks with anger in her eyes.

"Even though our loss was not great if we take into consideration the forces that have betrayed us. We are under-manned everywhere but the northern and western borders and those are already maintaining a light staff as they don't border demon territory. I have issued emergency redeployment orders so reserve units from the north, east, and west should arrive within the week."

"So a week to gather men then another week to move south giving Jin at least two weeks to plan and prepare for us." Releina looks even more distraught than before; all this grave news is not helping her.

She needs more time to cope. Normal people cannot get over losing family in just one night. She is pushing herself and running the kingdom will not give her much time to grieve. Letting the enemy prepare for that long cannot be good for us and the battle will be on their homeland, morale will be high. The princess most likely cannot lead the army, and Suzuki or I will have to stay with the princess. They could get a general from some other fort to lead the army, but how would they react to following the Princess's orders? Nothing good will come from that. They could look down on her for being a woman or still being young. I don't have a perfect understanding of the culture here yet. The general could in the worst case be sympathetic to the rebels and join them, and this needs to be resolved as soon as possible. There is only one answer, I had hoped that this information would open up a different path but we are not that lucky. Everyone looks to be in thought still. At least the enemy is doing us the favor of gathering together and not spreading out.

"Princess Releina." I raise my voice slightly and change to number 15, stern but respectful.

"Please give me the order and I will end this." Everyone in the room looks shocked except for Releina.

"I had planned on asking you to lead the army to suppress the rebellion, but it will still take a few weeks to prepare your forces. Also, Fort Armor is highly defended; laying siege to it will be difficult. Moving siege weapons will take even longer; I want to give you all the power we can muster before you move out." It seems she is thinking this through. However, she is missing an enormous part of the information to form a good plan of attack. She doesn't know much about war, even with this world's lengthy history it doesn't compare to back home.

"No Princess, just give me the order and I will end this. I will spare all those that surrender. There has to be a significant number of their forces that do not know the whole situation, and the faster we do this, the more we can save from being drawn into this conspiracy." If things continue the rebels will add common people to their ranks under the guise of local unity.

"Yes, that would be for the best as we will still need to defend the south after this. But the forces we have now will not be enough." I thought she would have understood me by now, but it looks like I have to spell it out for her.

"Releina-hime!" She pauses and looks at me, confused and blushing.

"I am your sword, wield me with conviction and I will end this. The enemies are normal humans, your world's conventional knowledge says that they have no chance against a hero who is meant to fight demons. So Releina-hime, give the order and I will end this for you."

"But Seigi-sama, how many would you have to...." I cut her off before she could voice that argument.

"Any that do not heed my words of surrender, all that still dare to oppose you will have resolved themselves to their fate. That is why I will go; not an army, not a subjugation force, a hero will tell them to lay down their arms. Any that will not surrender, will be ready for what they chose. So, once again, Princess Releina. I, Seigi, your hero ask you for the order to end this rebellion and bring back peace to your kingdom." Releina, now in tears timidly responds.

"Please Seigi-sama, end this tragedy." Mia then comforts Releina and escorts her back to her room.

"Sir Suzuki, I need a bit of information and equipment before I head out. If you assign someone to aid me that would be of substantial help, and I leave the princess's protection to you and Mia."

They have no hero and their assassins failed, their leadership is either going to fall apart, desperately struggle, pulling the kingdom down with them or they have foreign allies. No matter which of those is right, giving them time is bad for our side so I will use this time to see what my physical limits are.

As well as my mental ones, just how many lives will I take and how will they weigh on my mind if at all? Though thinking about all the people that will die as a simple test of myself, already shows how little their lives matter to me. My only desire at this moment is to not see her cry anymore. I will end this rebellion swiftly regardless of how much blood I will shed.

Common Foot Soldier

I'm Thomas, 19 years old and starting my fifth year of the first half of my required service. I am part of a normal military exercise on the outskirts of a tiny farming village I call home. Being deployed in the military isn't strange at all, even if the Southern Demon Lord hasn't revived. Their minions still attack human settlements occasionally. They act like wild animals when the demon lord is not around.

The low-level demons are kind of dumb, not like the demon generals and the demon lord, those demons can even kill heroes if they are not careful. Living in the kingdom is the best. We have food and water aplenty because the power of mana that the royals and nobles have is far greater than any other nation thanks to the heroes. Every ten years one of them descends from the higher plane and using their god-like power they fight back the demon hoards and bless people with their children, demi-gods that have mana rivaling heroes.

My parents are merchants, so they are some of the few people that leave the kingdom. I used to go with them when I was little and once the border is out of sight; you have to be very cautious of monsters, demons, and bandits as they could come out of nowhere to attack you. Mother has enough mana, so we didn't have to worry about bandits, but monsters and demons are a genuine threat if we go too far off the major roads. We were kind of poor so father pulled our cart, using magic he is as strong as pulling horses just nowhere near as fast. Mom defended us with wind magic until I was ten and my mana affinity manifested as fire. I had enough mana for elemental manipulation so I could make flames, fire scares monsters so traveling became easier.

Then I started my service and luckily my family had built up enough to start a farm in the southern territories. It costs a lot less because I was doing my service in the southern army, with that our family can be farmers from now on. My parents could not become farmers until now because they came from a destroyed nation to the west. That nation warred with the kingdom and lost, but their armies only killed the nobles and royalty; they did nothing to the common folk.

In fact, the kingdom gave anyone that wanted the right to move to the kingdom. If you were young enough, you joined the army, or you found whatever job you were good at before, like my parents. I was born here so I only know the tales my dad tells me about how bad their life was before and I pray the kingdom never goes through the troubles their old home went through. Since I entered the army everything has been going great. I am a scout so I am not supposed to fight demons only train for when the demon lord revives.

While my deployment is rather mundane and routine our current location is very troubling. My village isn't at the border with the demons or the one with humans, it sits at the edge of Archduke Aranwell's territory to the north. Where it connects to the rest of the Twilight Kingdom; there are only a few other territories between here and the capital. There are a lot of rumors going around about why we are here, but the only one that makes any sense is, the Archduke has rebelled. From what I have heard, no noble has ever done something like that inside the kingdom, so I don't believe it.

I don't get any of the political stuff that happens between important people. I've only heard good things about the king but I've lived under the Archduke's rule and I got to say; if they are at odds, the Archduke is probably in the right. I just hope there is no fighting; we have demons and monsters to fight already; we don't need to fight people too. Even if the Archduke demands six months of military service from each family every year not counting the mandatory ten years everyone in the kingdom serves, he is very fair with his taxes.

This means that one of my parents has to

serve as a reserve unit for half the year but reserves only fight when the demons invade. It's not like we are out there dying. Mostly we fix roads and bridges or guard for tax collectors. More importantly, it's thanks to this system that I met the boss and don't have to be a farmer like my siblings.

This is my fifth year serving, I met the boss in my second year. I was able to prove my worth and he'll accept me as a live-in apprentice when my tour is done. However, I don't think I'll get to take that opportunity now. This morning we got confirmation that there was a rebellion and we might have to fight any day now. They have put me on the front line, I'm not a skilled fighter but I am part of the supply chain for our scouts since I can use the flare spell and I can pass messages for other scouts. I've been expressly told not to fake an injury and lay on the floor as the next line has to trample any corpses in the way to keep fighting. I only hope that the fighting is limited and I can stay out of the way.

I've been deployed for six days at this campsite now, the main army showed up three days ago, the scouts have not reported any enemy movement. I can still hope that there will be no fighting. Dawn breaks on the camp and it is in a panic, a red flare burns in the sky. They have spotted enemies. I don't know how many, but they have flanked us. On a hill overlooking our troops in the east, I can vaguely make out a shadow as it catches the rising sun. That hill was a lookout post. Those people are likely dead if the enemy is there already.

"Attention, soldiers of Archduke Aranwell!" A powerful voice radiates across the battlefield. It shakes my heart and sends a shiver of fear down my spine. I've heard of a sound device that lets an entire city hear a person's voice, that must be what is projecting this person's voice. They are probably officially declaring war. The nobles like their pageantry.

"Archduke Aranwell stands accused of high treason against the Twilight Kingdom! His crimes include orchestrating a coup, colluding with foreign powers, and the murder of the King and Queen!" What? The King and Queen are dead? What's this about foreign powers? What about the princes, they are supposed to be strong, what happened to them?

"I don't know if you have been deceived or kept in the dark, but Archduke Aranwell does not deserve the trust of his people! For years he has been undermining the Kingdom, working with our enemies to make us weak!" The voice goes on listing a lengthy series of crimes, but I'm distracted.

Using a telescope I got a hold of from other scouts, I could see the figure on the hill. It's a handsome young man in all black, but that isn't important. What has caught my eye is the plethora of weapons scattered about and most importantly an enormous broadsword stuck in the ground. I might not have even started my apprenticeship yet, but I can still recognize that sword.

Boss kept talking about his masterpiece, a massive broadsword given to the strongest man in the kingdom, the Red Knight. The Red Knight is famous, he rules a large territory to the west, it's the most fertile land in the kingdom. He didn't make it that way; it was given to him for his exemplary military service. Even among the summoned heroes, his strength was unmatched. During the last war, he single-handedly annihilated entire divisions. The man on the hill looks nothing like the red knight, so the only reason that man could have that sword is if he killed him.

"If you lay down your weapons right now, you won't even be considered accomplices! It will be as if you never raised your hands against the kingdom and you will return to your normal lives!" My mind is racing but I hear that last part and I immediately removed all of my gear dropping to my knees. I can see a significant number of people doing the same, some people are even crying. What did he say while I was distracted?

"I thank you for saving me the trouble and sparing the princess the guilt of killing the innocent! Next, those of you who lay down your weapons now will be treated as criminals, but your lives will be spared!" Confusion spread through the camp, he worsened the terms, why would anyone... before I could finish that thought a wave of dread assaulted me and the morning dew turned to ice around me.

Everyone around me including myself is openly trembling. I've never been to a real battlefield, but I recognize this feeling from the stories old soldiers tell us newbies. This dread is a manifestation of that man's killing intent. More than half of us have now laid down our weapons or just fallen over after being overwhelmed by his killing intent.

"To those of you who remain standing, I applaud your devotion! If only it wasn't misplaced, you all would have made excellent subjects!" The man slowly walks down the hill. After a few steps his form blurs and he disappears from my line of sight, I can't see him anymore but he is still emitting that dreadful aura. I see an arc of blood to my right spray high into the sky accompanied by screams. Instinctively, I shut my eyes and cover my ears. I don't want to know what will happen, I don't want to see or suffer a hero's wrath. Try as I might the sound that fills my ears are nothing but the screams of pain and the splash of blood, lots of blood.

Archduke Aranwell

Even with all the mercenaries I could hire, more than half of my army is forced conscripts, new soldiers with little training. I planned on taking the field to bolster morale and keep them loyal. But I can't even do that now. This is too fast, way too fast. It has not even been a week since the coup began. How did she respond so quickly? How did that child muster a force to challenge me this fast; even a monster like her should not have been able to do this, I should have had another two weeks minimum. The armies could not have gathered this fast. Just what kind of miracle did she pull off?

Zara appears next to me. He is one of the assassins from the south, the only aid from them we currently have. If I could wait another month, we would have an army from them. However, the new hero is far too powerful if he awakened magic that could stop Mikeal this would have been pointless.

"My lord, we have spotted only the hero Seigi, he is making demands of the conscripts to surrender. There is no time to rally them now, all you can hope for is that they slow him down while we prepare the fort, with your army in complete disarray and no hope of regrouping that is all we can manage. The coup failed once Mikeal died no one but a hero could hope to defeat another hero."

I had planned to use this time to plan my escape. My allies don't have a hero with them but they still want to strike a blow against the kingdom, but that is foolish now that there are two heroes loyal to that monster of a princess. With my mana, I could be a king in any other nation in the world, if only I had time to run, but he is practically on my doorstep.

"So did you confirm that Mikeal is dead, not captured?" These assassins are good but they are not official troops from the south, that is why they are here far earlier than their armies. All of them are part of that guild in the south.

"From what we gathered, the hero slaughtered all the forces in the castle, there were no survivors. Also, the hero's mana is odd as you mentioned; we can detect him easily but not predict where he will go. I implore you to return to your fort immediately." Dammit all, at the very least I avenged my family's deaths with the king and queen's death, but it seems like rebellion is pointless now.

How did this go so wrong, all of my attacks predicted and countered, all the royals dead save the princesses and Mikeal dead along with most of my allies? According to the assassins sent from my allies abroad, the hero Seigi noticed them just as they began the operation and instantly killed their leader that was targeting the first princess.

Though the rest completed their mission, they barely made it out with their lives, they say. Did she do this? Is that monster playing with my heart again? Does fate favor her this much? I made sure nobody was targeting the younger princess so we would not suffer divine wrath by harming a saint. So how, how did everything turn out this horribly wrong?

The assassins will stay with me to see the mission to its end, but they cannot deal with the hero. Maybe if it was just the old man, but not Seigi. If that princess had sent a normal army they could have helped kill commanders or even the general but it is just that hero, that monster of a hero is cutting my army to shreds alone so they are useless to me now.

I don't think I can last till reinforcements get here; the fort is built to serve as a frontline base against the demons so it's possible I can hide in there but for how long; I thought I would have more time, dammit. I don't know how, but this has to be her fault, that monster's fault. I can just hear her laughing at me, no, laughing is beneath her.

Thomas

I don't know how long it's been since I shut my eyes and ears. I've been repeating children's stories over and over to pass the time and drown out the screams. A while ago something warm splattered on me, but I don't know what it was. It's getting cold and I'm hungry. But I won't get up. I won't even touch the rations in my pack. I properly surrendered, I can't let them mistake me for someone resisting so I continue to sit, repeating my stories. Suddenly, a hand is placed on my shoulder.

"You surrendered the moment I revealed the truth. Your loyalty to the crown will be rewarded. This wagon will take you to a nearby city to be processed." The voice from the hill just spoke to me. I practically jumped to my feet, but it's been hours so I wasn't ready. I stumble. The owner of the voice catches me. He has such powerful arms and a calming smile, I practically melt as that smile draws the tension from my body. But the smell of blood in the air brings me back. How is he not covered in it?

"Careful, you don't want to injure yourself." He helps me into the wagon. There are nearly two dozen of us crammed into this wagon. I recognize all of them, most are from the scouting party I was helping.

All of us have black stains, I wonder what that is. Did they mark us with tar? I hope it washes out. My military uniform is quite a bit better than my civilian clothes. The other passengers are talking about how kind the hero was. I guess that guy was the new hero, of course it was, who else could it have been.

It makes sense. Only another hero could kill the Red Knight. It sounds like we are being taken to a city where they will confirm our identities and pay our dues. Those who didn't surrender right away won't be paid their dues and will be put to hard labor. Their first task is to bury the dead. I am so glad I surrendered. I'm still not sure if the Archduke was in the wrong, but he lost and only the winners can be right. That is the will of the Gods.

Archduke Aranwell

The next day I finally received a report on the battle at the border. The hero was casually walking through the surrendered troops, not one of them made a move against him, not even the ones that did not surrender. When he encountered a soldier still standing or armed, he casually picked up a weapon dropped by a surrendered soldier and killed the armed individual. They couldn't even resist. He moves so fast that even my best soldiers only pointlessly blocked before his overwhelming strength crushed their stance.

He then left the blade in them and moved onto the next victim. The major general was trying to rally the rear forces but was silenced by a sword that flew so fast he couldn't even react. Not a single soldier was given time to suffer. A single powerful strike to the heart or head killed each one. Even those that resisted. He simply hit them harder, cleaving through armor and sword in a single strike. After the battle, some regular forces appeared with wagons. They took some of those who surrendered away. They forced the rest to clean up the battlefield. He may have spotted the surveying corps, but he just collected some weapons and left the battlefield toward the southern forts.

He can be here any minute considering how fast he made it to the border. Since this report got here first, he may not have come here first. The fort we abandoned; he could have gone there or he could be scouting the area around the fort to ensure we don't escape. That is it; the escape route that the castle knows, he might try to use it to infiltrate. I'm glad I had it sealed before this entire thing started. Unfortunately, we haven't finished the new one yet I needed those two weeks. Suddenly, a booming voice echoes through the fort.

"I am the hero Seigi, on Princess Releina's orders! Everyone in this fort is to disarm and open the gates." I am too late again.

Seigi

Dealing with the forces at the border was a lot easier than I thought it would have been. That little trick I picked up from those assassins helped, more than half of them ended up surrendering. And by the end, a few of them even just killed themselves rather than surrendering; they must have been very loyal to go so far, but ritualistic suicide was a tradition back home too, so it makes sense.

What is most surprising is that even after running around for almost the whole day, I have not gotten the least bit tired. Since coming here I have only been tried twice, and both times were when I used my magic. This entire event should have made me exhausted. I was running at close to my full speed for over 8 hours but nothing; I was only slightly hungry afterward. Oh well, I guess my body has changed more than I thought after coming here; I will have to stay observant of any negative changes that I haven't noticed yet.

Having made it to the fort that the rebel leader is supposed to be hiding in, I observe the area. No one seems to have noticed me. The fort to the southwest was empty, as expected. They also destroyed the emergency escape tunnel. I could not find a replacement so they might not have been able to complete it yet, another good reason to have done this as fast as possible. None of the people responsible for this will get out of here alive. Oh damn, I crushed another sword. Why does that keep happening? It's time to make my announcement and observe the perimeter.

"I am the hero Seigi, on Princess Releina's orders! Everyone in this fort is to disarm and open the gates." I wait to see if there are any responses.

A guard from a watchtower fires an arrow at me. I dodge it and respond with one of the throwing knives I took from that assassin's corpse. The knife hits the archer in the heart and they go down instantly; the strength I have now really is beyond human. Just how strong are those demons I am supposed to fight? I walk around the fort and set my face to number 11. In this situation it should be appropriately intimidating. As I circle the fort, the modern look of it surprises me. It looks almost like a warehouse district from my old world, but where there would have been fences there is a stone wall instead. The castle and castle city looked like pre-industrial era Europe, but this fort and the other look very modern and simple.

"I have captured or killed all of your reinforcements to the north. Anyone who surrenders will be spared, anyone who resists will be killed on the spot. I am only here to retake the fort and end the Archduke's life and the assassins that killed members of the royal family. As a hero, I do not wish to kill citizens of this country who have committed no crimes. I am giving you all until I complete my sweep of the fort's perimeter before I enter it and begin."

As I am walking around I attempt to seal the fort's doors with the throwing knives, based on the blueprints they showed me they open outward so this could work. Honestly, I am not putting much faith in this method, but I must do what little I can to prevent any of my targets from escaping.

Ok, that should be enough time, I put on number 15 and take a running start. I jump right over the ten-meter wall into the courtyard; I hear shocked gasps all around me. Then three arrows come sailing towards me but they are just too slow; I respond with throwing knives and dodge just like before.

There are five soldiers on the ground not holding weapons cowering and three more rushing me. They seem skilled but just so slow, I move in right next to one and pierce his heart then take his sword and repeat with the other two. Afterward, I check all the smaller buildings first and tell anyone who has surrendered to wait in the courtyard leaving their weapons behind. The remaining guards in the towers also surrender and go wait in the courtyard.

Finally, the headquarters or war room; the largest building in the back of the fort where the Archduke has to be waiting along with those assassins. I don't want to enter haphazardly, damage to the fort has been minimized so this should be fine. I make four large slashes along the west wall to make a new entrance. No need to walk right into a trap. I also seal the door the same as the others, down to just one more knife now. The sword I use shatters after cutting the wall, leaving me with only two more.

Surprisingly enough, the duke charges me right through the entrance I just made. Guess he decided to make a last stand. The wind surrounding him seems to already be formed into blades. That could be troublesome. I cannot get in close like this. I cannot have him waste my time. I need to find those assassins or the princess might not be able to move on. I used my last knife on him, there is enough room between the floating blades that it can get past easily, I hit him in the head and he dies instantly. Even his death gives me no joy or anything else either; these fool's deaths were meaningless to me, I find that annoying.

Upon entering the room I don't see anyone else here but I can feel the assassins' killing intent, they are still here. I don't want to move from the opening as they might escape. I have only 2 swords on me now so I can only throw 1. As I hesitate an explosion goes off along the outer wall, it must be a distraction so I pay it no mind, but then the other side of the room also explodes and an assassin lunges at me from the opposite side of the room.

I cut off his arm that was holding a dagger, then I noticed that he appears to have some kind of bomb strapped to his chest. I kick him to where the explosion just happened. Another assassin appears, they must have been using magic to hide, they catch him and proceed to suicide charge me with the two of them ready for death.

Looking at the device on the first assassin, I jump back and attack at a distance. After leaping away, I throw the sword I have at them; they explode. Now the entire room is on fire. I might have been able to withstand that explosion considering how strong my body is now, but I will not test that. The other two presences are gone and everything in the room is destroyed or on fire. It doesn't look like I will get any information on who those assassins were.

I have the men that surrendered put out the fire and I go outside to call for the recovery crew. I need to let everyone back at the castle know what happened here. If I had more practice with my enhanced abilities, I might be able to track them, but I have no idea where they went. They must have had an escape route already planned. Hopefully, this is enough to give the princesses closure, but if I ever find those two again. I will end them along with anyone else working with them.

Suzuki

"With the death of Archduke Aranwell and subsequent fall of fort Armor, and fort Helm which had been abandoned with a skeleton crew that surrendered, this rebellion has been quashed. Refilling these two forts won't be easy but with the reinforcements we already called back from the north and west; they should function until we can get back to proper numbers. It is a consensus among the nobles that your coronation will occur on your sixteenth birthday later this year. Until then you will act as provisional Queen with advisors appointed by a gathering of the high nobles.

The land from the rebelling nobles has been temporarily entrusted to the nearest loyal nobles with no increase in ranks. Upon your coronation, the land will be turned over to the crown and we can discuss how to handle the land after. No nation admits to cooperating with Aranwell and they all send their condolences for the passing of the King and Queen as well as pledges of additional support in case there is any movement in the south." The mood is very somber. The initial joy at the success of the mission faded quickly, replaced with the weight of how to deal with the future.

"Sir Seigi will return to the capital in two weeks' time, he is overseeing the handling of the surrender. The initial group will be paid from the Archduke's seized assets and will be offered the choice of continued service or returning to their homes. We have sentenced the criminals to hard labor, they will be divided and sent to farms to help, mostly in the former territory of the Red Knight.

This will free up hands to be conscripted to help fill the forts. Normally, after such a feat, there would be a parade to celebrate the Hero's triumphant return. Sir Seigi has personally declined, citing the necessity of holding a state funeral and the clashing mood expected between the two events. The funeral for the Royal family should be held as quickly as possible." Princess Releina looks to be taking everything far better than before. Right now she is focused on learning everything she needs to run the kingdom.

"I would prefer to wait for Seigi-sama to return before we bury mother and father," Releina spoke up for the first time in this meeting. Everyone appears troubled by her request.

"That will be fine, their bodies are already dressed and being preserved with magic, the extra wait won't pose a problem." Mia takes the princess's side. I don't think we have the mages to spare preserving them for weeks when all of our defenses are down, but I won't argue here.

"Very well, we will schedule the funeral for two days after Sir Seigi returns. That concludes the report on the failed coup. Return to your posts." Everyone gets up and leaves. There is a lot of work to do to keep the country running smoothly. I cast a glance at Mia. She orders Anna to allow the princess to continue sharing a room with her sister, then ushers her and the princess out.

"That was a rather abridged report of the battle. I received a report from Shanna, the maid, I lent him for this battle. I assume you wish to discuss the details. His actions, to speak nothing of his abilities, fall within my expected parameters. He was neither brutal nor cruel." I raise my hand to silence Mia as she goes on praising Seigi.

"Mia, do you know why there are such rigid guidelines for how to treat heroes, how to introduce them to this world and when to allow them to fight?" She has realized I have something important to say and is mulling over my question.

"There are different reasons for each of those, but I'm guessing you mean the last one. It has to do with what is recently being called 'capital syndrome'. The people in our capital live such peaceful lives, so divorced from violence and death that they have a hard time adjusting to life outside."

"That's close enough. Our world is so peaceful that it has become very difficult for a normal person to kill anything, especially other humans. Do you remember the Blue Knight?" Such a kind soul. That man hated the idea of hurting anything, but he was also a pragmatist and quickly understood the reality of this world.

"Yes, it was quite a famous rumor that he would cry into his wife's bosom after every battle."

"Do you know how many people I've killed?" I remember each and every one of their faces at the moment I took their lives. They don't haunt me because I had to kill them to protect someone else, but I can never forget their faces.

"You've led a very long and distinguished career, I couldn't imagine how many lives you've taken."

"Thirty-seven. That is how many of my fellow human beings I have slain, including the twelve from the coup. Most of them were easy. They had pointed blades at me or the princess, so

I had to respond. The hardest was like that boy outside of the safe room. People I am unsure if I should kill them. His face haunts me and it will for several more weeks. I won't be able to sleep for at least a month." I still remember the first one forty years ago. A soldier threatened Roland with a knife and I had to end his life.

"I didn't realize death affected you so deeply. But I understand the point you are trying to make but not why you are making it." I can guess what she is thinking by that angry look on her face, but she is missing the point.

"My point is that heroes are meant to fight demons, not other humans, that is why they have such limited engagement against other nations. People like the Red Knight who can take life without hesitation are an exception among exceptions in my world. That is why heroes have to be conditioned over months about how this world differs from our own. It is a hard thing to understand let alone come to terms with enough to learn to kill even if it is not a human. Now, how long has it been since Seigi was summoned?"

"Are you saying Sir Seigi is like that detestable mongrel?" There is ice in her voice. She has fallen for him hard. I wonder how he did that?

"Only in the most abstract way. The Red

Knight was a deviant, born defective most likely. I believe Seigi was created." She is confused. This is understandable, no one like him has ever been summoned before, I checked with the church.

"Before our world was peaceful, my homeland had a caste system not too unlike the one you have. The major difference is that the ruling class directly below what would be your king was a warrior caste. They were raised not just to rule their domain but to defend it personally. A duel between these nobles would even decide some conflicts. When the world became peaceful, these systems all over the world dissolved as gold became king and even later information.

My homeland had more trouble than others adjusting to the new world, which led to some major catastrophes the likes of which this world could not even dream of. Afterward, many of the highest-ranking families refused to give up the old ways, but they all vanished from the face of society. Turning to other avenues to preserve their power, some legal and others not, but what all of those families shared, their history, their traditions. Those were passed down regardless.

I believe Seigi is from one of these families. There is no other way to explain the ease with which he can take a life and show none of the common side effects of doing so, as the red knight or as

219

the blue knight. The sorrow that the blue knight suffered when forced to take another's life or the disgusting pleasure that the red knight had when stealing one's life. Either he has already taken life in our world or he has been raised such that it is expected of him. These seem like the most logical reasoning why he is the way he is and his actions so far support my theory."

"Does this make him dangerous? Should we warn the princess? Or try to separate them?"

"No, for these warriors honor and loyalty were absolute, and you heard him that day. He is her sword. A weapon meant to take another's life; to protect what is most important with deadly force." If my theory is correct I hate to think about what kind of childhood he had.

"This sounds like excellent news, but your face says otherwise."

"The Hero summoning takes people from all walks of life. Some mere children. Others well past their prime. While it would be difficult to describe any known hero as normal, they have all been of a fairly average background. The summoning strengthens them and is rumored to amplify certain characteristics. I don't know how someone like Seigi would be affected by the summoning. This might link back to the situation with his mana.

Other nations may view him as dangerous. I would prefer to keep his abilities hidden, but the current state of the world will not allow that. He may already understand this to some extent. If he reveals his power at the wrong time, it could turn our allies against us. We will have to build a narrative among our allies that show him in the most favorable light possible. While it hasn't been used in that way in this world, are you familiar with propaganda?"

"It's a method of disinformation to control the opinion of the populace. How is that going to help? Common folk already view the royals and heroes as demi-gods. It is hard for them not to when they can feel the enormous differences in mana. While the nobles have far more than common people, the difference between common people and nobles is half that of the difference between most nobles and royalty, and that is half the difference between most heroes and royalty. Taking Releina and Seigi-sama into account, the difference widens to unmeasurable levels. Don't you remember what the high priest said when he first saw Seigi-sama? That old man thought he was a god."

"None of that matters. It won't be our citizens we will manipulate but those of ally and enemy nations. They will see him as a threat and make moves to eliminate him, but if their people are against such action, it will limit their options to things we can deal with. Not that I think they could kill Seigi. What I am more worried about are the princesses; because of past tragedies. Those two are the only remaining royals.

This kingdom will only last as long as they do; that is what Sir Siegfried said when he was alive. 'The Twilight Kingdom is an anchor for humanity in this world and the royal family is its anchor,' that is what the first hero's queen said. So like him, I will ensure the royal family lives on for the sake of this world's future."

"I understand. We can use merchants and bards to spread rumors. We'll start with a romanticized version of these past events. A heroic tale of a knight fighting for a princess's tears. I wonder if she would be happy or embarrassed over this." Mia puts on a rather devilish grin.

"I'm certain both." My first smile in days spreads across my face. She will love this, he won't reject it, but if he reacts negatively at all, we must switch plans. I hope for her sake he accepts this role as well.

Foreign Spy

Hello there, I am the friendly traveling merchant Dex, at least that is who I am today. In reality, I am a top spy for the mercenary guild. I travel around all the human nations gathering information at the behest of anyone with deep enough pockets. Of course, I don't know who I am always working for, but unless they pay an extra premium, the guild can sell any information I get to anyone else anyway.

Today though, I will finally be able to get a good look at my current target of reconnaissance; the new hero summoned by the Twilight Kingdom. They summoned him two months ago, but there are some big rumors floating around the kingdom about him. First, is that the eldest princess is completely infatuated with him and it might be mutual. I heard that they had spent almost every waking hour together for his first few weeks here. Love, at first sight, sounds too much like a fairy tale to me. They only parted because of that incident and even then it was entirely because in his eyes it was an abhorrent affront to her. He could not let it pass.

Second, he single-handedly crushed a rebel army of over five thousand men and took most of them prisoner. He then proceeded to get revenge for the princess by killing the leader of the attempted coup and all his assassins. There are some unsubstantiated rumors that during said coup he also killed the kingdom's previously most powerful hero, the Red Knight Mikeal 'Ash' Romanoff, who was in league with the conspirators. If that one ends up being true then this kingdom's military power would, in theory, go up from what it was before the coup as the new hero easily outclasses any known hero in the world or history, aside from this kingdom's first, the 'Hero King.'

Today is the day of the public funeral for the former king and queen and the new queen's older brothers. That reminds me the hero saved the oldest princess at the same time that all of her family was being killed, so he prioritized her life over theirs. That supports the narrative that is all the talk today. Unfortunately, all my information is second hand as I could not see him yet or even confirm his name. But that is to be expected, honestly, this much information on a new hero this soon after summoning is unheard of, the royal family normally has them sequestered for months undergoing secret training.

Ah, the gates are opening up. Time to get to work. I can get a good spot thanks to my merchant connections. I should be close enough to get a good look at him and his actions. That is normally all I need to judge a person, I still do my due diligence gathering information but it always just confirms my initial theory, I am an expert judge of human character. The new queen is making some kind of speech.

She is desperately trying to hold back her tears and keeps glancing at her right to reassure herself. I guess she is just as in love as the rumors have said. She doesn't look as young as I thought either, wasn't she still a child? No, it says here she should be 16, but she looks older, I guess royals mature faster. Actually, if I remember right, my boss told me that everyone in the kingdom matures fast because they don't lack food like most other nations.

The hero must be to her right, she announces, the new hero, Seigi, her sword? Sounds like he has pledged himself to her fully. This entire event seems way too mushy for a funeral. But the crowd is eating it up. People are crying both tears of sorrow and joy, I would not be surprised if this was also a wedding. The queen appears to be stepping aside. It looks like Seigi will say a few words. I can finally get a good look at him. Well, he looks the part, tall, well built and his face seems like.

Wait? What is wrong with me I cannot breathe; the instant I look upon his face my blood runs cold, my face is pale, my spine tingles, I become light-headed, and yet remain calm. This is abject terror, a feeling I am very familiar with. Why am I so terrified? He doesn't look threatening. He is not radiating any killing intent; he doesn't even appear to notice me; I am just another face in the crowd, what is going on.

I cannot rationalize this feeling of terror. The only thing a little bit off about him is that his face seems to be fake. But that would make sense; he is new to this world and dealing with this kind of huge public event most people would put on a mask even the princess earlier had one on. My mind cannot unravel what my body is telling me with every instinct I have built up to this point. That hero is not human, he is a monster. The last time I felt like this was when that earth-dragon appeared out of nowhere in those tunnels, but that made sense, it was a dragon.

If I cannot explain this feeling, how can I put it into my report, this doesn't make any sense. I can surmise that his power is real from this feeling, but that alone doesn't explain this. Why I am afraid, why I am sweating so profusely, why do I feel like I am about to die, why can I not stop trembling? No, I am still not breathing, get a hold of yourself man you have been in much worse situations before this just remember those demon scouting missions.

Control your body, breathe in and out and again, focus your mana and force your body to move. Wait, what is going on? People are panicking, did I miss something, the hero said something and everyone looks calmer and everyone is leaving the castle grounds. The hero is escorting the queen back into the castle. It seems in my panic I missed something important.

"Hey buddy, what just happened did that hero do something scary?" I ask some guy near me.

"Huh, what, you were right here, did you not hear? Demons have invaded the east, Fort Wing is already under siege. The hero Seigi will leave within the day, all to protect the kingdom for the queen. Everyone is leaving so we can prepare, there will most likely be a call to arms; even the hero cannot defend the whole eastern front."

"The whole eastern front, not just Fort Wing?" That is not how the demons normally attack; they follow patterns and attack specific points in waves unless they overrun a fort.

"You didn't hear anything, did you? That was why everyone was scared. Over one hundred thousand demons were on the march through the mountains. Every fort on the eastern border will be under siege within a weeks' time some might even be overrun so the villages closest are being evacuated."

I am in shock. One hundred thousand demons. I have never heard of an invasion force that large. I did not even think there were that many demons to the east. This report will have to be a rush. I have to get back to the 'Free Cities' and spread the word; if the demons are acting differently, the worst case is this kingdom is done for. This is no time to be worried about that creepy hero. The border for demon territory could change for the first time in a thousand years.

Conversation Far Away

During the same time that the Twilight kingdom is being invaded, in a castle far to the south, well beyond the demon territory at the center of the continent, on the most southern part of the continent back in human territory. A youthful man with a dark complexion walks over to a modest throne with another youthful man sitting on this throne. His handsome face dimly lit by a torch to his side makes his bronze skin glow. There is a difference in station between these men, easily determined by the quality and make of their attire. The man walking is in a military uniform while the one on the throne is clad in royal purple robes but is lacking a crown. This is a castle on the border between Sow, the largest southern human nation, demon territory and the monster nation of Mu.

"Sir Zabi, our forces to the north are prepared to move. How is the report from our assassins?" The military man stands at attention eagerly waiting for his marching orders.

"A failure." The royal on the throne does not hide his anger or displeasure but remains seated and calm.

"But those were our best men, what happened? The assassin's guild has never failed us before, this is terrible." The military man shows his youth by breaking his stance once he hears the unpleasant news. The two men share a familiarity that goes beyond their station, so neither is thrown off by the other's slight disregarding of proper etiquette.

"I just got the report so I will have Zara give it again." The royal waves his right hand, signaling to someone in the shadows.

"Zara, why him?" Again the military man's youth and inexperience are on full display as he cannot contain his shock.

"Just listen, little brother, it will all be explained." Zabi motions his hand and a very slender man with black hair, black eyes and black skin emerges from the shadows. His clothing appears to be simple rags, but on closer inspection, all the extensions of cloth are on purpose to blur his form while running, making targeting him near impossible.

"Sire, everything was going according to master's plan. The southern nobles had come to the Archduke's side with the goal of revolution.

Never has the royal family been this weak, and they were ready to make their move. He was even able to bring the red knight over with fake promises of giving him the princess. That knight did not even realize that we had to kill her or the castle itself would have killed all of us. Master had decided to just give him the younger princess if he ever figured it out, but that never came up.

The Archduke easily got us into the castle as low-level servants; our trouble began once we activated our acceleration magic. The one point where we thought we had unimpeded freedom. Activating that magic was the signal to begin the operation, so the red knight moved to seal the door to trap both of the other heroes in the room. But once the red knight's back was turned and moments before we completed our mission. A flying sword impaled master. We could not even see the attack. It and the attacker were nothing but a blur to us.

It was only after our master was dead did we realize that it was the new hero that had thrown his ornamental sword with enough force to splatter his corpse on the wall and shatter the sword. In that same instant, the white knight grabbed the princess and made his way out the window. We who remained continued our mission and killed the rest of the royal family, but since the princess was still alive, the throne room began to magically seal all exits, not just the main one that the red knight had sealed with his magic.

With our acceleration over, master dead, and the princess alive, all we could do was flee as we would have to wait days before we could use that spell again. If our master had lived, he could have used it again and fought alongside the red knight, but the rest of us were spent. We could only hope the red knight could deal with the rest in the castle. So the four of us fled to the southern fort that was the rendezvous point. Once we arrived we heard that all of our forces had been repelled, as if all the key points had been secretly reinforced just before our attack. The red knight had fallen at the hands of the new hero and all the invading forces in the castle purged.

The Archduke quickly made plans to bring as many men to his side as he could, but most of the other nobles had already pledged themselves to the new queen or at least were keeping neutral. The new hero invaded the Archduke's territory only three days later, not even waiting to gather an army to assist him. That option was never part of our plans, and the Archduke could not convince any other nobles to rebel with him because of the swiftness of the hero's counter-attack. He did not even have time to marshal all the forces in the south. He was left only with the standing army that had been marshaled beforehand for military practice drills. Those troops were not even ready for a rebellion if he had time, he might have been able to force their compliance but the hero was far too fast.

His voice alone brought about fear and terror to the Archduke's forces at the border; half of them surrendered without even fighting, then he released his killing intent. Another fifth of the army fainted at its weight and it froze most that remained in terror. The hero did not even have to release mana to invoke that kind of fear. While we could not get close to him, from what we could tell his mana has a terrible weight to it. The waves it created with his killing intent alone is a weapon, soldiers weaker than the kingdom's might have died from it alone. Then it began. The hero stormed through the battlefield, assassinating all who still carried a weapon by plunging his sword right into their heart, then taking their own weapon to use on the next.

After a few hours over a hundred of the remaining soldiers standing gathered themselves enough to take their own lives after having to watch their friends and family die at the hands of the hero. During the entire event, the hero looked to be pained by the situation not taking an ounce of pleasure in his duty however he did not look like he was under duress either, I can only say he is a perfect warrior. His face told that he was doing his duty, and these men needed to die, he had no ill will to them and none to those that gave him the order. The perfect soldier.

Because of the swiftness of this battle the retreating forces that had attacked other points in the kingdom never made it back to the Archduke's territory they surrendered to local forces before ever getting to the south. Archduke Aranwell called all of his remaining forces to Fort Armor. He only ended up with around five hundred men before the hero arrived.

The hero gave the same speech to the fort as he did to the border army while walking around the perimeter of the fort in the open. Only one archer gathered the courage to fire at him during this time; he dodged the arrow and returned the attack with one of master's throwing knives right in the archer's heart. Death was instant, the blade pierced his heart but the force of the impact broke his spine.

I doubt even our master could have hit that same target from that distance, let alone still have it be lethal, and repeating that kind of damage is impossible. A few of the men dropped their weapons after his speech. Still, no one moved to open the gates, but then the hero leaped over the fort's walls, shocking all those who saw. I retreated to the Archduke's side while he was still in the air since our escape route had been secured earlier. Less than an hour later the hero had captured the fort and only the command room remained; we had an ambush prepared, but it did not matter the hero cut through the wall instead of coming through the door.

Archduke Aranwell in a panic rushed him clad in all of his various magic but was felled by a single knife between his eyes. Completely overwhelmed, we tried to distract and injure the hero with bombs. Vic charged at him, but the hero noticed the bomb and removed Vic's arm and then kicked him away before detonation. Shin then rushed to catch Vic and the two of them again lunged at the hero with the bomb. Kara and I activated our acceleration and fled. We heard the bomb go off prematurely, so I doubt they were successful in even injuring him. We finally got back here only moments ago using the secret tunnel through demon territory."

"This is a monumental loss, three of our top assassins and a five-year plan up in smoke." The man in a military uniform is forlorn as he gazes at the ceiling in disbelief.

"Rei, as you just stated, the plan is a failure. You are to have your forces stand down. No need to plow through demon territory now. I will figure out what to do about this disaster later, both of you are dismissed. Zara, our contract is finished. The two of you go report to the assassin's guild of your master's death. We will probably not bother with the kingdom for a while, so the two of you are free from my retainer. If I have another job for you, I will contact you the usual way."

The two men exit the room leaving Zabi alone with his thoughts, after some time a silvery mist flows out from behind Zabi's chair and coalesces into a beautiful woman in a very revealing one-piece red dress that expertly accentuates her ample bust and hips. This strange woman takes a seat on Zabi's lap and wraps her arms around his neck. He places one hand on her leg and another around her waist. Then speaks to her with a somber face on.

"Carla, what do you think about all this? You lost one of your best students, two of his students, and your plan is in tatters. We will have to start over from the beginning if I am to have a chance at the throne." Carla moves in and rests her head on his shoulder, also resting her chest on his. The two of them embrace and she responds.

"Honestly I am terrified, to think one hero could have made a complete mess of our plan has astonished me. To the point that I truly doubt that it was just the doings of one hero that so expertly ruined our plans for the future." Zabi has a look of shock come across his face and he pulls her in tighter.

"Do you mean we have been betrayed?" Carla strokes his face with her hand to calm his worries as she makes herself comfortable on top of him.

"No, based on that report I think we may have run afoul of someone else's plan in addition to underestimating the new hero. Now, who do you think has benefited most from our failures?" She smiles at him devilishly while asking that question.

"My eldest brother's faction, but how could they have interfered?" Carla's face becomes sour, she pinches his cheeks while responding.

"No, you're thinking too selfishly, just like a child. Who in the Twilight Kingdom is now the most powerful person there?" Carla moves her face right in front of him and looks into his eyes while he ponders this question even farther. She is now straddling him, sitting on his lap and holding his face in front of her. After a few seconds, the idea pops into his head.

"The first princess, with only her younger sister alive she will be queen; a position that would never have been given to her before our coup."

"But how could she have done this?" Carla again smiles her devilish grin and answers him.

"I think it was a happy accident for her, a string of events just falling into place for her. If anything, it looks like we helped her more than she did anything herself." Zabi has a confused look on his face as he holds onto Carla sitting on top of him.

"I am not following; accidents and we aided her? How do you reason that?" Carla pulls his face into her chest as she explains.

"First, the extra defending force at all key positions in the country just might have been her troops preparing for their own coup. Second, the new hero saved her life instead of the other royals. Just looking at that you could make a logical leap that he cares for her, and I can think of a few ways that could have happened so fast just after his summoning. Then, we have the hero's strength exceeding all expectations." Zabi adjusts his face slightly inside her cleavage, his face is beet red though there is no embarrassment on his face.

"So you are saying that she was planning a coup of her own and we just acted first, gifting her the crown." Carla adjusts his robes, moving them down slightly.

"Now you get it. There are other possibilities, but none that make as much sense. Say that the king knew of the coup and placed extra personnel at those key points himself. Why did he not have more people guarding him and his family, and why did he have them all come back to the castle? No, the most likely scenario is that the first princess wanted the throne and had been preparing to take it for some time.

By chance a powerful hero falls into her lap, possibly literally, expediting her plans. After that we assassinate her family for her so she never has to dirty her hands angering the nobles and the people. After that, she has just reason to unleash her new pet on us to clean things up." Zabi looks up into her eyes as she is talking to him but makes no move to remove himself from between her warm ample bust.

"If that is true she would be quite devious and very lucky to have the crown so neatly wrapped up and given to her." Zabi's face is getting redder by the second.

"Either way, she is incredibly lucky because even if everything else was according to plan, her being alive is only because of the new hero." Carla continues to push his robe down his back.

"Yes, plans dealing with that kingdom will not work anymore, we will have to make inroads locally or even at home if we are to make any gains now." A trace of gloom passes through Zabi's eyes, but only for a second as Carla moves his face up out of her cleavage and closer to her face.

"If that was all we need to talk about I will take my payment and leave you to think. I have warmed you up enough that it should taste exquisite."

With that, the beautiful woman bends down to Zabi's face and begins kissing him deeply. While his hand moves all over her body, one settling on her rear and the other on her breast. She lifts her head away slowly, he is completely red. Then she moves to his neck revealing her fangs and bites into him softly, he grips her tighter as she begins to slowly suck his blood from his blushing neck. Moments later he releases her, and she finishes with another kiss and seals the wound on his neck. She gets off of him and turns into mist again, while her form melts away her parting words are.

"I will be waiting, for once you are king I will be your queen and we can continue where we left off. I promise you my wisdom and power along with this form you desire so badly."

Zabi is left alone in his throne room once again, to plan for the future, a liter lighter than before and fully drained of his mana.

A Story From The Past

I'm Misumi Makoto. I am a very lucky person. Having graduated at an awkward time, I had almost no job prospects. But my senpai went on maternity leave and put in a good word for me at her school. It may be a bit out there but it is not like I am in the middle of nowhere, it is a small private school just outside of the city. Now I get nearly an entire school year with her class; a chance to get to know the students and affect them. They are a typical sixth-year class, smaller than some bigger schools, but I should have an easier time learning about all of them.

She left some notes on each of her students; it seems she had this same class when they were in 5th grade. Small private schools can do things like that. There are the usual troublemakers, a few diligent or quiet ones and a hyperactive yet sweet one, your typical average class. It would be a perfect class, if not for two problems. They aren't big problems, but they are enough to make me uneasy on my first day.

First, is the boy in the back window seat, it's kind of funny that the students in that seat always seem to have the world revolve around them. However, senpai's note says he has no friends and to leave him alone, he passes all his tests perfectly so don't upset him. That's horrible, senpai said, he is the perfect student and very mature for his age; it is her opinion that he is simply a late blower and will reach out when he is ready.

I thought senpai was a better person than that. You can't just abandon a child like that, this is their formative years, they could make friendships that last forever. His silence is likely a cry for help. Having minored in child psychology, I have to do something for this child.

I've already got a plan to make him everyone's friend just like I was back in elementary school. The second problem is even less of a problem, but it worries me more. Being the type of person to over-prepare this one is a special problem for me. I'm getting a transfer student at the end of my first week. It's technically a wonderful thing, a brand new friend to integrate into my class, but I won't have senpai's cheat sheet to help me understand this student.

The worst part is I won't get any of the child's files until the day before the transfer, something having to deal with privacy and security. I don't remember other schools having this level of security, though; I had to have a detailed background check done for this job. For my peace of mind, I need to solve my first problem before the second one gets here. Don't worry, little boy, sen-sei will help you out.

My first day was more awkward than I would have liked, but the children responded well. I'm very confident in my "friends plan". I left a note on his desk to see me in the office after school, so we could talk in private and I can get to know him better. I wonder if it was cowardly to start like this, but I never had the chance to talk to him during class. I was going to talk to him but he was very focused on the work that was given and I only have one class with him today. Sen-pai was right though he is very mature for his age, he already looks like a modern businessman very serious and he finished his work right on time not earlier or later he was done right before the bell.

"Makoto-sensei." I jump when he calls my name. I was too deep in my thoughts and he sur-prised me from behind. I am totally not afraid of a little kid, no matter how scary his eyes look, all devoid of emotion.

"Senpai, uhh, your last sensei, told me you don't have any friends in class. What about last year, have you had any friends while at this school?" He doesn't change at all. He looks into my eyes, trying to read a deeper meaning from my words. He is really mature for his age.

"That's right." He flatly states. He is fairly intimidating for a child. Why do I feel like I am talking to my boss?

"Well, I thought up a plan for you to make friends in class. I would like if,"

"No, thank you!" He interrupted me, causing me to jump again, he raised his voice slightly. Which drew the attention of some other teachers in the office, but they only glanced over before getting back to their own work.

"I think it's a good thing to get along with the other students." His eyes look me over completely as if judging me, then his gaze returns to my eyes. I cannot tell if he is being rude or polite. There is no intent in his gaze so I don't think he is looking down on me, if he was older I might have thought he was checking me out, that was the gaze he just gave me. It is making me uncomfortable but there is no reaction on his face at all, just what is he thinking?

"I get along fine with all the other students, on our last group project I was the lead and everyone worked together well. Just because we aren't friends doesn't mean we are hostile. My current status is fine, no one has an overly negative or positive opinion of me from what I gather; everything is within the margin of error." The certainty with which he speaks makes me question if what I'm doing is even right. No, I'm the adult here, I know the importance of making friends and learning how to get along with others. They taught us that a child isolated from their class will do worse in class and life. I need to do this. For his sake, for his future.

"Still, I want you to make at least one friend this year. Think of it as a challenge to your intelligence. I am sure you can do it if you try. Making friends while you are young is a significant benefit to your future. You may even find your partner among the other children." He looks me over again, silently judging me like he is wondering if I really have his best interests at heart. This feels weird. A child should not be able to look into your soul like this. He feels almost like an old priest looking at me like I am the child here.

"I understand, if that is required, I will try. Now if that was everything, I need to head home, goodbye sensei." He turns to leave and I feel like a weight is lifted off my chest. I think something went wrong in our conversation but he is on board so let's implement my plan. Although I may have to think of him as having a far more mature mentality than before, that is likely why he has no friends. He could be one of those geniuses that don't get along with normal people, a savant maybe? Arg, I wish I took more classes in psychology now.

Later that week I got the file on my transfer student, weirdly some of it was blacked out none of the other students had information blacked out, weird. Tomorrow she will start in my class. I only have tonight to prepare for her. Oh, and my other problem seems to be, growing? It didn't quite go as I expected. I called on him in class and I paired him up with the other students as often as possible over the week and even assigned homework groups. Unfortunately, though, it seems to have had the opposite effect. The class now seems to be wary of him and it just gets worse every day, I would not say they fear him but it is almost there. Let's put that aside.

My transfer student is the most adorable little girl. Her smile is like rays of sunshine just washing over you. The notes from her previous school say she is very shy and withdrawn, but she got along well with her classmates. It took a long time for her to warm up to them and forcing the issue will cause her to withdraw further. So it's a wait and see with her. I don't think she will break through before summer, but she should be fine before she graduates. The only open seat is next to him, but I don't think that will cause any problems, right? What could possibly happen?

It's a miracle. My new little angel descended upon the class and enacted a miracle. She started with the impossible. She spoke to that boy. And now they are friends. It was already defiance of fate for her to speak to anyone on her first day. But to call what happened over this week as anything less than a miracle is an insult to my angel. I saw her speaking to him in the quietest of whispers in between each class. He looked aloof and disinterested at first. But now they are walking to and from school together, it's surprising that they live near each other, this has to be fate I know it.

Neither of them speaks up in class unless prompted, but they have opened up to each other and they always eat lunch together. Even with his stoic face still unmoving I can tell that they are getting along just fine. During the last week I heard her discussing plans to meet over the summer. It is just the most adorable thing ever. They look like two little lovebirds. My angel is perfect, it is a genuine Beauty and the Beast story.

Summer vacation was far too long and too short. I was kept away from my angel forever, but I never got more than a few days' rest as I was constantly busy preparing for next semester and securing a job after this one. All of that's behind me now. The second semester is in full swing and nearly all of my worries are gone. There's only one worry left, and it sounds more like paranoia than a genuine worry because I lack any proof. I think my angel is being bullied. It seems to have started right after the summer break but I haven't been able to find proof it's happening or of who is doing it. Let alone why.

My angel is so sweet that she would never say anything bad about any of her classmates. While I'm sure that boy would say or do something, he appears to have taken the stance of, if she doesn't say anything neither will he. I tried to subtly hint that there was bullying going on and it needs to stop. Unfortunately, I think I made it worse. Now I'm not lacking in evidence of it happening.

Every day her shoes are misplaced or vandalized. Her desk and belongings are treated similarly. But I can't figure out who's doing it. All the other students are in solidarity. I'm afraid of asking him. He might know who it is but his eyes get scarier every day, that glare of his that once held no emotion is slowly being colored with the burning light of wrath. I might not be cut out to be a teacher, you are not supposed to fear your students; you have to help them.

It finally happened. My angel came back from the restroom soaked head to toe, sobbing silently. Her parents were called in and she ended up transferring schools. I was worried about how he would take the news. I planned on catching him at the gate and comforting him, but he was talking to my angel so I hid. When she left, I went with my prepared words of comfort and encouragement. He glared at me with a frightening intensity; I backed away instinctively. I couldn't speak or move. I was like those deer caught in headlights waiting for death. After a moment, he whispered.

"She was crying." He left school grounds, but I was frozen for a few more minutes. He did not raise his voice but the way he said that last word filled me with terror as I have never felt before. His unchanging gaze was full of rage like he would explode at the slightest provocation and I just could not be the one to set him off.

I'm scared. I'm scared for the students involved in the previous bullying and I'm scared for myself, but he is only ten. Why am I feeling like this? I don't know if I'm just working myself up over nothing, but that boy's eyes scare me. The target of the bullying shifted to that boy after my angel left. But he came to class and put his wet shoes on the front desk and glared harshly at each student as though saying to everyone 'this is unacceptable'.

Two of the girls broke out into tears and one of the timid boys offered him their shoes. He declined and wore visitor slippers the whole day. I think I now know who was bullying. It's a group of two girls and four boys. I still have no proof, but they look at him with the same look of worry I have. He has done nothing to them and I don't think he will, but still.

Each day as he makes his way to class he gives them a glare that clearly says 'I know it was you'. It is making the boys angry, and the girls scared. He's given me that look a few times. I think he holds me responsible for not stopping it, I know it should have been my job to stop them but I didn't know who it was. I overheard that group plotting something. I didn't hear specifics, but I heard some dates.

I told my fellow teachers and that boy. He's always watching them now. The teachers seemed to not want to get involved either, all of them were worried about him and some teachers had him when he was younger. They never had a problem with him before, it seems he has always acted mature for his age and the other teachers just left him alone like my senpai said to do. They crowd now even normally deserted areas when he walks through them. Though they were reluctant, the principal and vice-principal had everyone pay closer attention to him. Hopefully, this is enough to atone for my previous action. I hope he thinks it's enough.

The worst thing possible happened. No, this is far worse than anything I could have imagined as the worst. When I heard the commotion, it was already after school; all the students should have been gone, I rushed over as fast as I could. Hoping an adult's presence would end whatever was happening, I raced over to the park next to the school. I arrived as he swung a large stick down at one of the bullies, silencing his muffled cries. I don't know how to comprehend what I'm looking at. An enormous crowd is making it look like an arena or fighting pit all the kids are just staring at them. That's what you would describe it as based on the outcome at least.

Several other adults got here before me, yet did nothing to stop what was happening. That boy is breathing heavily and has a scrape on his head and a few bruises forming on his arms. If not for the bruises I would think he just finished a long run and had tripped. He looks just like he does every day as he walks into the room or lazily stares at the board. It's those eyes, they send a chill down my spine. How can he have such eyes even after having done all this? All 6 of the bullies are on the ground unconscious and bleeding.

The boy he hit is bleeding from his head and the fingers on his left hand look like a large rock crushed them. The offending rock is off to the side, covered in blood. One of the girl's legs is bent at an angle that legs shouldn't bend. The other's face is so swollen you wouldn't normally be able to recognize her. There are teeth all over the floor. I'm guessing from the girl with a swollen face and the boy whose mouth is a bloody mess. The other one has it worse.

He's bleeding from several wounds and his arm has swollen yet still doesn't hide the bone poking through. The last boy is the only one without an obvious injury. He's in the fetal position, holding himself. I can easily guess what happened here. They attacked him, and he retaliated. I'm sure any witnesses would back up this claim. But this level of brutality is unnatural. They are just children. How did it end up like this?

After that incident, the school was closed for a few days. Instead of classes, students had mandatory counseling. I sat in on all the students from my class. They all said they expected this to happen. They were instead shocked that it wasn't that boy who started it. For the few who saw the scene of brutality; some of them were worried they would face something similar because they didn't stop them from bullying my angel.

The psychiatrist says I'm doing a good job getting the students to be open, but I know I'm a failure. All the students knew who was bullying, but they didn't think I could help so they kept quiet. Wallowing in my self-pity and guilt, I don't notice the next student come in until.

"Sensei." That uncharacteristically characteristic way of speaking. I panic for a moment, thinking I've been caught off guard in an alley or something. The psychiatrist notices my unease, I'm sure she is evaluating me as well as the students. Normally I greet the students and introduce them to the psychiatrist, but I'm a nervous wreck, and cannot seem to say anything. I cannot even look him in the eyes, staring at the ground I feel his gaze silently judging me.

"Have a seat young man, we're going to discuss the events of the other day. Is that ok?" True professionals are a godsend. She got the boy to sit in front of us, then I noticed her writing something onto her clipboard while looking at me.

"Can you please tell us, in your own words, what happened, from start to finish. Every little detail that you can remember." He gives a confused look to the psychiatrist then glances at me before returning his gaze to her before responding to her question.

"Do you mean that day? The specific incident? Or from the very beginning?" The psychiatrist is shocked to hear this from such a young child, I told her before he is very mature for his age. He speaks like my college professors giving a lecture to the students who didn't understand it the first time.

"Let's start with the incident and then cover from the beginning." She responds calmly, and the boy nods his head as though he would have chosen the same.

"I was attacked, and I defended myself." That is how he summed up that level of brutality?

"That's it?" The psychiatrist looks shocked and confused. He delivered that line like he was answering a question in class. Giving only the exact answer with no superfluous information, as if the entire event doesn't matter at all anymore.

"Without the context, anything more wouldn't make sense, it would simply be stating the events not why they transpired." What is with this boy? I knew high school students who were not this articulate.

"Then could you share your story from the very beginning? I want to see it from every angle."

I'm interested in his side as well, I've heard from all the other students, even the victims. How does he view what happened, where does he place the blame? Contrary to our expectations of the story starting like everyone else's, after the summer break. His story starts at the very beginning.

"It started when we got a new teacher for our homeroom class." My mind is reeling. It started with me? How? I missed a bit of his story, but I caught the part that confused me.

"She ordered that I make a friend." That's what this is, I forced him to interact with the other students that caused the friction, but then he made a friend.

They targeted her to get to him. But he would have ignored my angel if I hadn't demanded he make a friend so she would never have been targeted. She probably would have been treated exceptionally kindly after having been rebuffed by him. He's recounting the weeks of bullying that occurred, but I cannot hear any of it. I had always assumed it was indirectly my fault for not stopping it but I would have never considered it was directly my fault, from the beginning it was me. While nothing else is getting to me, three words cut through my confusion and panic like a blade of ice in my heart.

"She was crying." These are the only words I've ever heard him speak with any emotion. It's the same blood-freezing emotion he said to me when she left. I can't even spare a glance at the psychiatrist to see what they think. He's begun recounting that day. I missed everything in between.

"They approached me on the way home from school, in the park right off of school grounds. They taunted me. Saying, 'We made your little friend go away. Now you're alone like you should be, you creep.' I ignored them, intent on getting home to finish my schoolwork. When I tried to walk past them they grabbed my backpack and tried to take it from me.

When that failed they spoke more taunting words and punched me in the face. I fell. Then I realized this was finally my chance; they wanted me to retaliate; I saw no reason not to. I looked around for what I could use as they kept hitting me. Once each of them had hit me at least once, then I defended myself. They hurt her, they hurt me, so I hurt them." I interrupt.

"But that was too much; that girl's face and the other's leg, that boy's mouth and the other's arm, how could you? Those kinds of injuries may not even heal right, was that your intent?" I could

257

not help but raise my voice, but luckily I was able to prevent myself from yelling or crying.

"I wasn't wrong. Everything was fair, my response was within reason for what they did." For a second his eyes shine with that rage once again and I recoil instinctively. The psychiatrist looks happy for some reason, then they respond to him.

"All right, young man, I have heard everything I need. You may go back to your parents now. I will give the principal my report and he will send it to them." He leaves while I'm still in shock. The psychiatrist is scribbling lots of notes. I try to start a conversation to shake the fear out of me.

"What did you think of him?" I can barely get those words out of my mouth.

"He was fascinating! When he first described the event I was expecting at least residual anger at having been attacked. Or if your evaluation of his intelligence was, then indignation at how he's been treated like a criminal. In the worst-case, pride in his accomplishment of beating six opponents at the same time. But nothing was present, nothing of any kind. He spoke of the event with complete indifference, as if it happened to someone else long ago.

I was worried he had an antisocial person-ality disorder, but he doesn't show the coping signs of a high functioning sociopath and did you catch that emotion when he spoke of his friend leaving. He has some kind of disorder resulting in his awkward display of emotions, but I cannot place what it is exactly with only one meeting. He will have to attend the required regular therapy, I will have to work with him till I can form a proper diagnosis. But whatever he is, he should still be able to be a functioning member of society once I am done with him."

The psychiatrist seems pleased to have found someone strange. It's rather gross. We're done for the day so I leave them to their scribbling notes. I'm packing my things in the office, won-dering if I should reconsider careers. When that familiar voice comes from behind me.

"Sensei." My blood runs cold. I turn to see him standing in the doorway. He steps in and shuts the door behind him. I jump a little when it closes. Looking around, no one else is here; the office is empty but others should still be in the school somewhere, why is no one here?

"Sensei, I wanted to ask. Why did you do nothing?" I've never been more afraid in my life and of a child no less. I'm trembling, but his gaze seems to hold me and forces an answer out of me.

"I didn't know who was responsible. I had no proof." That answer escaped my lips while my entire body trembles.

"No proof, is that necessary? You saw what was happening and did nothing." His response is like a dagger in my heart.

"I did not know who exactly, I only had a feeling, neither of you said anything. I am not an all-knowing god." He stepped forward and spoke again.

"Then if I could get her to talk, it would not have ended like this, she might be fine and I would not have had to deal with them." Deal with them? He doesn't even think of them as people, does he?

"Deal with them? Is how you see it, what you did was extreme! They didn't deserve what you did!" I raise my voice, but I keep from yelling.

"They made her cry." He looks confused again. How does he look at people like that, like they are nothing?

"What you did was wrong! You don't even look remorseful about it! You did not look angry then either, and they were terrified, I was terrified!

How could you do all that, with that 'face!' Are you some kind of 'monster'; what is wrong with you?! You, you, demon!" Halfway through the conversation, I started yelling. I am trembling. He still has his calm emotionless face staring at me not reacting to his teacher yelling at him.

"A monster, they called me that too. And my face, what is wrong with my face? I was born with it, I cannot change it." I cannot move, frozen by fear, but I cannot stop myself from responding.

"That response, that way of talking, every-thing about you is terrifying! It is not 'normal' it is not 'human' it is like you truly are a 'monster' or a 'demon' it is not natural. That scares people, you are too different!" I have been screaming this whole time, why has no one come back? Are they scared of him too?

"Ah, so that is what you mean. I am differ-ent, too different from everyone else. Thank you, sensei, for the explanation. This is starting to make sense. So it is how I did things, and how I looked doing them that was the problem. How-ever, what I did was not wrong! That was Justice!"

He looks like he has made some kind of epiphany and I swear it looks like his eyes are glowing with the light of the setting sun. Just then, when he said the word justice, the smallest emotion crept into his eyes again. They were burning with rage. After that he turns to leave without saying anymore to me. When the door slams shut I collapsed to the floor. I won't come back to work tomorrow. I cannot handle this kind of stress. Leaving my resignation letter on the principal's desk; I leave the school for the last time. I think I need to take a walk. If I remember the park next to the school has a path that goes on for a good while.

Printed in Great Britain
by Amazon

45150375R00156